Seth Hardy made her reckless.

The sane part of Taylor told her she should forget him. He was too hard. Life had dealt him too many blows. But part of her was intrigued, and that side of her said, *run to him,* take every chance in the world.

She had never behaved like this, never thrown herself at anyone, never awakened in the night gasping from dark, sensual dreams.

Seth gave her no encouragement. He said a relationship was too complicated. He kissed and made no promises. Even if they made love, she knew there would be no guarantees about tomorrow.

And yet she wanted to go to him. Now.

Dear Reader,

Welcome to Silhouette **Special Edition** . . . welcome to romance. Each month, Silhouette **Special Edition** publishes six novels with you in mind—stories of love and life, tales that you can identify with—romance with that little ''something special'' added in.

April has some wonderful stories in store for you. Lindsay McKenna's powerful saga that is set in Vietnam during the '60s—MOMENTS OF GLORY—concludes with *Off Limits,* Alexandra Vance and Jim McKenzie's story. And Elizabeth Bevarly returns with *Up Close,* a wonderful, witty tale that features characters you first met in her book, *Close Range* (Silhouette **Special Edition** #590).

Rounding out this month are more stories by some of your favorite authors: Celeste Hamilton, Sarah Temple, Jennifer Mikels and Phyllis Halldorson. Don't let April showers get you down. Curl up with good books—and Silhouette **Special Edition** has six!—and celebrate love Silhouette **Special Edition**-style.

In each Silhouette **Special Edition** novel, we're dedicated to bringing you the romances that you dream about—stories that will delight as well as bring a tear to the eye. And that's what Silhouette **Special Edition** is all about—special books by special authors for special readers!

I hope you enjoy this book and all of the stories to come!

Sincerely,

Tara Gavin
Senior Editor
Silhouette Books

CELESTE HAMILTON
Single Father

Silhouette Special Edition

Published by Silhouette Books New York

America's Publisher of Contemporary Romance

For Robert, who shared Alaska with me.

With special thanks to a pilot named J.D.,
whose cocky grin made me ask
the age-old writer's question, "What if...?"

And to my parents,
who gave me a haven where I could fill in the blanks.

SILHOUETTE BOOKS
300 East 42nd St., New York, N.Y. 10017

SINGLE FATHER

Copyright © 1992 by Jan Hamilton Powell

All rights reserved. Except for use in any review, the reproduction
or utilization of this work in whole or in part in any form by any
electronic, mechanical or other means, now known or hereafter
invented, including xerography, photocopying and recording, or in
any information storage or retrieval system, is forbidden without
the permission of the publisher, Silhouette Books, 300 E. 42nd St.,
New York, N.Y. 10017

ISBN: 0-373-09738-1

First Silhouette Books printing April 1992

All the characters in this book have no existence outside the
imagination of the author and have no relation whatsoever to
anyone bearing the same name or names. They are not even
distantly inspired by any individual known or unknown to the
author, and all incidents are pure invention.

®: Trademark used under license and registered in the United
States Patent and Trademark Office and in other countries.

Printed in the U.S.A.

CELESTE HAMILTON

has been writing since she was ten years old, with the encouragement of parents who told her she could do anything she set out to do and teachers who helped her refine her talents.

The broadcast media captured her interest in high school, and she graduated from the University of Tennessee with a B.S. in Communications. From there, she began writing and producing commercials at a Chattanooga, Tennessee, radio station.

Celeste began writing romances in 1985 and now works at her craft full-time. Married to a policeman, she likes nothing better than spending time at home with him and their two much-loved cats, although she and her husband also enjoy traveling when their busy schedules permit. Wherever they go, however, "It's always nice to come home to East Tennessee—one of the most beautiful corners of the world."

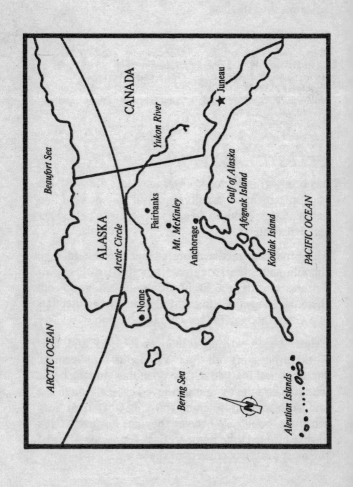

Prologue

The living room was bare, stripped of its well-worn furniture, its colorful throw cushions and its forest of green plants. The morning sun, which once had dappled the creamy walls with mellow tones, now ruthlessly exposed every crack, every smudge, every cobweb. But Taylor Cantrell ignored the flaws. She closed her eyes and took a good, deep breath. The scents of oil paints and dusty books remained. This was still her mother's house.

"I do that, too, you know."

Opening her eyes, Taylor found her father in the doorway. His hands were shoved deep in his jeans pockets, voice soft as he continued, "I can walk in this room and pretend Holly is here."

Taylor nodded. "Even after two years..." She swallowed, afraid to say more. She had promised herself she wouldn't become emotional today. Her father didn't need that. He was selling the house, remarrying, getting on with his life. As he should. He was a young man, really. He deserved more than memories of her mother. Holly would want more than that for him. As did Taylor.

Joe Cantrell came toward her. "It's okay if you're sad, you know. This was our home. It's difficult to say goodbye."

Meeting his warm, blue-eyed gaze, Taylor managed a grin. "I've never been able to hide a thing from you, Dad."

"I never wanted you to."

They smiled at each other with the mutual understanding born on a cold winter's day twenty-three years ago, when Taylor had strayed from her mother's side on a busy Chicago street and Joe had rescued her from the traffic. He had rescued both of them, really, by marrying Holly a few months later. The three of them had formed a perfect family. No problems at all—until Holly's car skidded on a stretch of ice and she died in the resulting collision.

Sadness, intensified by this empty room, engulfed Taylor. She didn't understand why the loss of her mother was hitting her anew these days. In the beginning, she had been strong—just as Holly had taught her to be. Strong and sure of herself. But lately, at odd moments, her grief was more acute than ever. She wanted so desperately to talk to her mother. Just once more.

Joe cleared his throat and pulled a book from the pocket of his tan Windbreaker. "This is something I think you should have."

Puzzled, Taylor took the book from him. The word Diary, scripted in fading gilt letters, decorated the front.

"It's your mom's."

Taylor opened the broken clasp, turned to the first page. The handwriting was her mother's and yet it was different, too, almost childish.

"It was in a box of old books up in the attic," Joe explained. "Not hidden, just mixed in with the others."

"Have you read it?"

"Yeah . . ."

The hesitation in his tone made Taylor look up. "What's wrong?"

"I felt guilty reading it. It's about your father."

"You're my father," Taylor insisted, as she'd been doing most of her life.

Joe grinned. In a familiar, affectionate gesture, he brushed a strand of light brown hair from her cheek. "Sure I'm your dad. I'm the one who paid for your braces and taught you to drive. But there was this other guy . . ."

"We went through all of that when I was about fifteen, remember? You and Mom tracked him down, found out he was dead. He had no siblings and I was his only child—"

"Yeah, you know all the facts about him." Joe tapped the diary Taylor still held open to the first page. "But he comes to life in here. Your mother started this journal when she was only sixteen. She writes a lot about her home in Alaska. And about *her* dad—your grandfather."

Taylor's gaze drifted back to the diary. She turned another page.

"You know she never said much about him," Joe said. "Nothing good, anyway."

Taylor sighed. "I know."

"After the accident, I thought about trying to find him. But she had told me so many times that she hated him. She was so adamant about it that I never pushed the issue. And when she was gone...well, I was so lost those first months without her...." Joe paused, his blue eyes dark with remembered pain. "I had good intentions. I mean, no matter what, I thought the man should know his daughter was dead. But I didn't do anything about it until I found this diary. And now..."

Taylor waited expectantly, half sure of what he was about to say, half afraid to hear it. "Now?"

In answer, Joe placed a crumpled slip of paper across the opened diary. A curious blend of defiance and uncertainty in his eyes, he said, "That's your grandfather's name—Gerald Austin. And that's his phone number."

"You called him?"

Joe nodded. "I think he'd give the world to hear from you, Taylor."

Minutes ticked past while she stared down at the name and number. Years ago, after Taylor had satisfied her curiosity about her father, she hadn't pushed for many details about the family her mother had left behind in Alaska. Taylor had all of Joe's family to satisfy the need for grandparents, aunts, uncles and cousins. But in the past few months, with her mother dead, with no sisters or brothers, she had realized there was no one else in the world who was truly, *physically* a part of her. That knowledge in no way lessened the love and respect she had for Joe or for his family. But she had all these questions, questions only her mother could have addressed. Now it seemed some of the answers were literally in the palm of her hand.

She picked up the slip of paper and closed the diary. "You think I should call, don't you? Even though Mother hated him?"

Joe met her questions with a steady gaze. "Taylor, I've never overburdened you with advice. I didn't have to. Your mother always said you were born knowing what to do. And you're twenty-five years old. This is up to you."

"But I'm asking for your advice."

"Then read the diary," he murmured. "You'll understand everything better after you read it. Then I think you'll want to call him."

Taylor and Joe shared a long look. "Okay," she said at last. "I'll read it."

"Good." With a last touch to her cheek, Joe turned. "Come on, there's some stuff in the garage I thought you might want."

Taylor followed him.

It wasn't until that night, when she settled down on the sofa in her own apartment, that she opened her mother's diary and began to read. Only then, as Joe had said, did she begin to understand....

Chapter One

"...and I never knew I'd miss the mountains. I wanted to see tall buildings and busy streets, but once I did, then I missed my mountains...."

Her mother's diary open in her lap, Taylor glanced out the airplane window. There were mountains below, great jutting peaks of gray and white. Her mother's mountains? Perhaps.

Only moments ago, the captain had announced they would soon be landing in Juneau, Alaska. And it was somewhere outside the city, on one of the many rivers that streamed off the glaciers and mountains, that Taylor's grandfather lived. It was there that her

mother had grown up. There that Holly had learned
to love *her* mountains.

The plane's engines thrummed, and Taylor could
feel the change in altitude as the craft began its descent. Soon she would come face-to-face with Gerald
Austin, her grandfather. Swallowing the lump that
rose in her throat, she slipped the diary into the oversize tote bag at her feet. She took out a compact, ran
a brush through her shoulder-length hair and fresh-
ened her lipstick. Then she wrinkled her nose at her
reflection, scrubbed off most of the lipstick and closed
the compact with a snap.

Would her grandfather think she looked like her
mother? There were obvious similarities—the hair that
was neither blond nor brown, the hazel eyes, the generous mouth. But Holly had been a dimple-cheeked
beauty, with a verve that shone from within. Taylor,
with the discriminating perception of an artist, knew
she hadn't her mother's sparkle. She was attractive,
yes, but not in a way that would make people look
twice when she passed. Maybe her grandfather would
be disappointed.

That was hard to imagine when Taylor remembered Gerald Austin's happiness the last time she had
talked with him. They had stayed on the phone for
well over an hour. In the six weeks since she had first
read the diary and decided to call him, there had been
many such conversations. The day she had told him
she would come for a visit, she was certain he had shed
some tears of joy.

Thinking of those tears made Taylor surge to her feet when the seat belt sign switched off. The plane was filled with tourists, hunters and fishermen eager for a few days amid Alaska's natural summer beauty. Belongings were pulled from overhead bins and beneath seats. In addition to her tote bag and carryon, Taylor collected a portfolio from the steward in the front. The square, zippered case was so large that it fit beneath her armpit and then hung midway down the calf of her leg, making for an awkward journey down the jetway. She was struggling with her load and irritated by the grousing of those behind her by the time she made it to the gate. Eagerly she looked around for a "tall, skinny drink of water with white hair"—her grandfather's description of himself.

He wasn't there.

Taylor regarded herself as a sensible person. She didn't panic unnecessarily. But for a moment, just one moment, she was desperately afraid her grandfather wouldn't show up. All around her, her fellow travelers were being met by tour guides and representatives who were calling out names and holding up signs. Taylor knew a second of aloneness, the same hollowness she had often felt since her mother's death. Then she shook it off. Telling herself that her grandfather was running late or she just hadn't seen him yet, she swung around, apologizing again as the portfolio slammed into people on either side of her.

"Taylor Cantrell?"

Relieved to hear her name called through the crush
of people, Taylor spun around again, excitement re-
placing her disappointment. "Grandfather? I'm
right..." Her voice trailed away as she realized it
wasn't Gerald Austin who had spoken.

The man who threaded through the crowd toward
her had eyes as gray as the mountain peaks she'd seen
from the plane. Gray eyes, framed by black lashes, set
in a face where handsome features warred with the
stern set of a masculine jaw. He wasn't a young man—
silver glinted in his thick, dark hair, and lines creased
the tanned skin around his eyes and mouth. Yet he
wasn't old, either. There was solid, male strength in
the hand that took the tote bag and carryon, and in the
other hand that fell to the small of her back and urged
her through the crowd. He was exactly the sort of man
Taylor had visualized when she thought of Alaska. He
looked ready to wrestle the elements and win. He was
so...*alive.* Yes, that was the word. He was bursting
with vitality. And because he took charge so quickly,
she didn't question who he was.

Once they reached the side of the corridor out of the
crowd's way, he lifted the bags as if judging their
weight. "Do you always travel with this kind of
load?"

His abruptness startled her. "I wanted to make sure
I had enough supplies—"

"Supplies?"

"I'm an artist."

His gaze slipped down her in a measuring way, his eyes narrowing with what Taylor could only describe as suspicion. Yet why shouldn't he believe her? She was about to ask for her grandfather when the man muttered, "Gerald said you paint or something."

"That's right." She frowned, realizing she still didn't know who this man was. "Excuse me, but I don't believe I caught your name."

He stooped to pick up the bags once more. "Sorry I didn't introduce myself first, but you caught me by surprise—"

"Surprise?" Taylor echoed, not sure what he meant.

He didn't explain, but said, "I'm Seth Hardy." He smiled—briefly, woodenly.

She recognized the name. "You're Grandfather's partner, aren't you?"

His nod was slight. "Have you got more luggage?"

"A few pieces," Taylor admitted, and wasn't surprised when his mouth tightened.

"Then let's get going."

He headed down the corridor toward the baggage claim area, his long strides leaving Taylor to scurry after him, the portfolio again flapping against her leg. She wondered why they were in such a hurry, but there wasn't time to ask.

Once her bags appeared, Seth made short work of loading them onto a cart and wheeling them out to a small van. A yellow-and-blue insignia with the words Austin Eagle Lodge was painted on the vehicle's side.

While Seth piled her belongings inside, a cool, misting rain began to fall.

Wishing for something more substantial than her navy knit stirrup pants and cream sweater, Taylor shivered. It felt more like March than the second week of June. She shoved her portfolio in back and climbed into the passenger's seat. Her grandfather had warned her that it rained frequently in southeast Alaska, that June could be cold and damp. But only a short while ago, as the plane circled above the clouds, the weather had appeared balmy. Now a low veil of fog and clouds shrouded the surrounding mountains, and the rain blurred her first real glimpse of Juneau.

The mist had become a downpour by the time Seth disposed of the cart and slid behind the steering wheel. Water glistened in his close-cropped hair and on his bright yellow slicker as he wiped damp hands on denim-covered thighs.

"I guess you're used to rain," Taylor said in an attempt at conversation.

He grunted in reply and started the engine. His silence continued as he navigated among the tourist buses and hotel vans that clogged the parking lot.

Taylor glanced at his chiseled profile and tried again for a response. "I expected my grandfather to meet me. Is he waiting at his floatplane?"

Cold, gray eyes swiveled to meet her gaze. "He couldn't make it to the city today. I'll be flying you out to the lodge. In *my* plane."

"That's right," Taylor said. "You own the float-planes that ferry guests out to the lodge, don't you?"

"Yeah." Again those eyes studied her. "Disappointed?"

Something in his regard made her straighten her shoulders. She didn't know what this man's problem was. "I've waited all my life to meet my grandfather. I guess another hour or so won't matter."

"I meant, are you disappointed that I'm the one who owns the planes?"

Taylor frowned, not understanding why she should care one way or the other. "Does it matter?"

After giving her another long look, Seth made no reply and concentrated on guiding the van through moderate afternoon traffic. Thoroughly puzzled by his attitude, Taylor switched her attention to their surroundings.

The city seemed to her to have been built on the lower slopes of the mountains. And after living her entire life in and around Chicago, she thought it felt more like a small town than a state capital. The bit of reading she'd done before leaving home had explained that the city was founded during the gold rush era in the late 1800s.

As the van paused at a stoplight, she turned to ask Seth if gold was still mined in the area, but the expression on his face made her swallow her words. He was looking at her with distrust—pure distrust. For Taylor, who had spent most of her life liking and being liked by almost everyone she met, the sensation was unsettling.

She decided to tackle the problem in her usual direct way. "I think I must have ruined your day, Mr. Hardy."

"Why do you say that?"

"Well, you don't seem too pleased that you had to pick me up."

His answer was no answer at all. "I pick up folks at the airport several times a week."

The traffic light switched from red to green, and Seth wheeled the van into a parking lot near the water's edge. He got out, slamming the door before Taylor could think of anything more to say. Through the rain, she could see a small structure at the end of a planked walkway. The building bore the same insignia as the van, as well as the additional inscription Hardy Air Excursions. Beyond the cabin, two floatplanes bounced on the water, and a couple of massive cruise ships were docked in the distance. Above it all were the mountains, hovering over the city, climbing into the clouds.

Taylor felt her excitement return. She was going to a place unlike any she had ever seen. A place her mother had once loved. A place where her grandfather waited. Even the unfriendliness of her welcome party wasn't going to dampen her spirits.

A sharp tap on her window roused her from her thoughts. Seth Hardy glared at her through the drizzle. "Come on. Let's get your stuff inside. I want to get out of here before the weather can get any worse."

Taylor got out, grabbed her portfolio and dashed up the walkway. A gamine-faced teenaged girl met her at the door and handed her a rain slicker, which Taylor donned before following Seth out to get another load. By the time she came back in, he had dumped the suitcases in the corner and was on the radio behind a counter, getting a weather report.

The cabin was warm after the chilly dampness outside, and smelled of freshly brewed coffee. The teenager, who introduced herself as Allison, gave Taylor a steaming mug of coffee and a smile of welcome. "We've all been wanting to meet Mr. Austin's granddaughter."

Taylor cocked an eyebrow in Seth's direction and murmured, "Not all of you, I think."

Allison giggled. "Oh, he's just grouchy 'cause the fog seems to be settling in. There's a load of tourists up at the lodge that has to be back in for their cruise ship to sail tonight."

"I thought most people stayed at the lodge a night or two."

"Some, but not all," Allison replied, going on to explain that in addition to overnight guests, they booked day trips for visitors who were treated to a flight over the nearby glaciers and a grilled salmon lunch or dinner at the lodge. In five minutes the girl had answered half the questions Taylor hadn't thought to ask her grandfather and hadn't dared ask Seth.

His voice soon broke into their conversation, however. "Allison, could you take some of Miss Cantrell's stuff down to my plane?"

Grinning good-naturedly, the girl departed. Taylor drained the last of her coffee in preparation for leaving. She was aware of the scrutiny of the man behind the counter, and tried to ignore him. But she couldn't. Finally she just returned his stare. "Mr. Hardy, I wish you would tell me what I've done to irritate you."

"I'm not irritated."

She gave an exaggerated sigh of relief. "So you treat every new arrival this way? It's an interesting approach for someone in the tourism field."

He shrugged. "I'm not into idle chitchat. Besides, you got all the information you wanted from Allison, didn't you?"

She blinked in surprise. "Excuse me?"

"Details about the business."

"I was curious."

His smile was tight. "Curious about our operation here. I notice you didn't ask anything about Gerald."

Taylor stared at him blankly, still unsure of what he was trying to imply. "I assume my grandfather and I are going to have plenty of time to get acquainted."

"Yeah," he murmured, his lips twisting bitterly. "Sure. You've got plenty of time."

Taylor didn't know why those words would cause his face to harden so, but he looked more foreboding than ever. She didn't get it. If he were just any other obnoxious person, she would ignore him. But this was her grandfather's partner. He lived at the lodge, and from what she had gathered from her grandfather about the living arrangements, she would be hard put to avoid Seth Hardy for the next six weeks. So it was best to get to the bottom of his antagonism right now.

"Back at the airport, you said I surprised you. What did you mean?" she asked.

"You just don't look the way I expected."

"And how was that?"

"Obvious, I guess."

Her frown deepened. "Obvious how?"

"Like someone coming to claim her inheritance."

His words shocked her into silence. He thought she was nothing more than a fortune hunter. The idea was almost too ludicrous to believe. Taylor opened her mouth, ready to deny his charge, but no words formed. Even if she had thought of something to say, she doubted Seth would have given her a chance to protest. Without another glance at her, he picked up some suitcases, banged out the back door and down the dock toward the plane.

Taylor stood immobile for a moment. Then, with mouth set, tote bag slung over one shoulder and portfolio clutched under her arm, she charged after him. She'd be damned if she would even attempt to explain herself or the reasons for her visit. This cold, judgmental man wouldn't believe anything she said anyway. She was going to ignore him. After all, she had come to be with her grandfather—he was the only person that mattered.

Seth stood at the floatplane, one foot on the bottom pontoon, another on the wooden dock, loading the suitcases Allison handed him. He kept his balance despite the slight up-and-down movement of the plane, oblivious to what Taylor saw as the very real possibility of slipping into the water. Avoiding his gaze, she passed him the portfolio and tote.

He shoved them inside and held out his hand. "Come on. You can climb in over the pilot's seat."

Taylor started to comply. Then the plane bobbed and she looked down. The water looked very cold and very deep.

"It's no big deal," Allison said encouragingly. "Just take Seth's hand, put your foot on the step beneath the door and he'll help pull you up and in."

It really was no big deal, and Taylor had never in her life been afraid of the water. So she held out her hand, felt Seth's strong, callused fingers wrap around hers, and she looked up, ready to take the step into the plane. His gaze stopped her, however. Cold and flinty gray, the look in his eyes made her hesitate. Her foot missed the step, and she felt herself begin to fall. Before that could happen, however, Seth jerked her forward, an arm encircling her waist, hugging her close as they both fell against the side of the plane.

Taylor clutched at Seth's wet slicker, her feet fighting for a purchase on the pontoon beneath them. The plane bobbed more violently than ever.

"Be still," Seth growled.

She complied and let his body accept her weight. Her feet stopped sliding. The bobbing slowed. She sagged with relief and her face pressed into the damp flannel shirt revealed above his slicker's zipper. He smelled of rain, of shaving cream and of the not-unpleasant musk of an active man. She breathed in those scents, even as she realized how she and Seth were situated—with his legs slightly bowed and her hips fitted intimately, tightly against his. She pulled away, looked up, and for half a heartbeat their gazes held. An awareness sparked between them.

He shattered it. "Get hold of the wing support," he muttered. "Then for God's sake, hold on."

The disdain in his voice angered Taylor. It wasn't her fault she had slipped. Determined to behave as her usual independent self, she grabbed the wing support and used it as a brace as she stepped up and into the plane.

Laughing, Allison applauded. "Way to go, Taylor. Most of our female tourists spend a little more time swooning in Seth's arms. He's one of our main attractions."

"I didn't swoon," Taylor protested, flushing.

Face stony, Seth climbed into the pilot's seat. "Allison, cut out the cute stuff and cast us off."

The teenager continued to laugh, even as she obeyed his orders, leading Taylor to believe that Seth's stern manner was a facade, ignored by those who knew him. He slammed the plane's door, and Taylor could see a muscle working in his jaw as he put on a headset and started the engine.

So females swooned in his arms, did they? She could understand that. He certainly cultivated the tough-guy image so many women found intriguing. Taylor was glad she wasn't one of those women.

The thought hadn't left her head when Seth reached around her, grabbing both ends of her seat belt. Again they were close, much too close for comfort.

Taylor took the seat belt out of his grasp. "I can do this myself, thank you. I am *not* one of your swooning fans."

"Good." He gestured to the headphones hanging from a hook beside her. "You might want to put these on. In case I need to tell you something."

She doubted she wanted to hear anything the man had to say, but she put the headphones on anyway. And then she and Seth were off, the plane pulling away from the dock and out across the gray, choppy waters of the harbor.

Taylor ignored Seth—not an easy task in the confines of the small plane. But excitement again replaced her irritation, excitement that mounted as the plane gathered speed and lifted off. And once more, Taylor was above the mountains. Mountains, rivers and eventually, ice.

"Glaciers," Seth explained tersely into the microphone attached to his headset.

Taylor stared down at the miles and miles of frozen blue that tumbled down mountainsides and up valleys. The glaciers' surfaces weren't white and smooth, as she had always imagined, but scored by deep, sapphire crevices. She longed for her sketch pad, even though she wasn't sure her skills would ever be enough to capture the wild beauty of the scene below her.

The sheer space of it all was what amazed her. Juneau was far behind them. For miles in every direction, she saw no other sign of human habitation. No houses, not even boats or other planes. The aloneness was exhilarating, and though she had vowed not to speak to Seth Hardy again, she couldn't contain the "Magnificent!" that broke from her when he dipped a wing and soared over still another field of ice.

Seth couldn't have heard her, not over the sound of the engine and the wind, but she was certain he knew what she was feeling. For when their eyes met, there was again that sense of awareness, of understanding. It was different than the moment they had shared when he had clutched her to him at the dock. And yet it was the same. They were communicating on a level deeper than words. Why that was possible with this unfriendly distrustful man, Taylor couldn't begin to imagine, didn't want to understand. She turned away from him, intent once more on the sights below them.

"The lodge is up ahead," Seth muttered, breaking into her thoughts some time later.

Taylor sat forward, heart pounding. Ever since reading her mother's diary, she had been imaging how this place would look. Ever since calling her grandfather, she had wondered about him. Could the lodge possibly match her romanticized notions of stone fireplaces and rough-hewn timber walls? Would the man be half as grandfatherly, a fraction as warm and welcoming as he sounded on the phone?

By the time the plane made a smooth landing on the river and taxied toward the shore, Taylor was clutching the seat belt strap and peering through the rain. She could see smoke from several chimneys, and a line of floatplanes drawn up to the dock. Two yellow-slickered figures waved exuberantly as Seth guided the plane to a stop.

This time Taylor ignored Seth's outstretched hand and bounded out of the plane, taking deep breaths of the spruce-scented air, her eyes drawn to the surrounding mountains. It was all as she had expected, and yet so much better, so much more beautiful.

The two slickered figures were shaking her hand, welcoming her, but it was a man at the end of the dock who claimed her attention. He was tall, in keeping with the trees and the mountains behind him. Beneath the hood of his blue poncho, Taylor glimpsed white hair and a lined face, a frailer man than she had expected. Yet so familiar. Especially the eyes. As she walked closer, steps quickening, she could see he had her mother's eyes, the same hazel as her own, yet brighter, brimming with the luminous, gentle humor that had been Holly's most special quality.

"Grandfather?" Despite Taylor's best efforts, the word caught on a sob.

And he caught her. Tears mingling with the rain on his cheeks, her grandfather caught her in his arms.

"It's so good," he whispered. "So good to have you home."

Home. At that moment, Taylor couldn't question the rightness of his choice of words.

A log fell in the fire, and the flames sent light dancing over the faces of the two people bent close together on the couch. From the comfortable depths of an old leather chair, Seth sipped his coffee and took a moment to notice the similarities between the woman and the man. The resemblance was unmistakable, extending beyond bone structure and coloring to the laughter that filled the room.

She's either genuinely happy to be with him or a consummate actress, Seth decided as Taylor once again laughed at something Gerald said.

Seth's instinct and experience told him she was acting. For Gerald's sake, however, he wished Taylor could be as sweet and as lovely as she appeared. Gerald deserved a granddaughter who cared more for him than for the tourist-rich business he had built in this Alaskan river valley.

And maybe Taylor would care for Gerald. Maybe Seth was wrong about her. Setting his coffee mug on the table beside the chair, he spared another glance at the woman seated beside Gerald. Seth had been jumping to conclusions about her ever since she had called over a month ago. He hadn't shared those conclusions with Gerald, of course. His old friend was too eager to know his granddaughter for Seth to diminish her in any way. At least without proof.

So Seth had been glad to fly into Juneau this afternoon to pick her up on his own. He had waited in the airport for her with a chip on his shoulder and a righteous fire in his belly, determined to take her full measure.

She had surprised him. At least at first.

He had expected an artificial-looking little tart. Not the slender, pretty woman who had stood in the midst of that airport crowd, her eyes big, trying to hold on to all the junk she was carrying. Seth had wanted to be nice to her. His affection for Gerald had stopped him, however. Gerald was ready to accept Taylor sight unseen, so it was Seth's duty to be a bit more questioning. For why, after all these years, after all the letters Gerald had sent to his precious Holly, why had Taylor finally decided to get in touch with him? She and her stepfather had told Gerald they knew next to nothing of him until a diary of some sort of been found. Gerald believed them. Seth had his doubts.

And the doubts won out over any softening in his attitude. Taylor Cantrell might not look like a mercenary schemer, but Seth had been fooled by a woman of her type before. He wouldn't again.

Those thoughts propelled Seth from his chair. He crossed to the fireplace and viciously prodded the logs with the poker. It wasn't until the blaze was crackling once more that he looked up and found Gerald and Taylor staring at him.

Gerald spoke first. "Seth, you're as jumpy as a bear cub fishing for his first salmon."

Seth seized a convenient excuse. "I'm wondering what's keeping Josh so late."

"Josh?" Taylor questioned.

Seth swung his gaze to hers. Gerald had talked so much about Holly at dinner that no one had mentioned Josh. "He's my son. He's sixteen—"

"Going on twenty-five," a voice cut in from the doorway. Everyone turned as Millie Rogers entered, bearing a tray with a cake protected from the rain by plastic wrap. Seth sprang forward to close the door against the cool damp air.

Graying and plump, Millie had been at the lodge longer than Seth and his son, longer than anyone save Gerald himself. She was a plain and plainspoken woman, with a heart as big as this wide-open state. To Seth's way of thinking, she was a credit to her gender.

He took the laden tray from her and placed it on the brass-trimmed antique trunk that served as a coffee table. "Josh will really be sorry he was late when we demolish this cake."

"Humph!" The older woman snorted. "If you go eating whole cakes, you really will be adding a spare tire, Mr. Seth Hardy."

He patted his flat belly. "Never happen."

"A lot happens when folks start gettin' old."

"Old?" Seth echoed. "Who're you calling old? I'll have you know I'm still breaking hearts in Juneau." With the ease of long-standing affection, he kissed Millie's still-rosy cheek.

"You're a devil," she retorted. "That you are."

Over her head, Seth's gaze met Taylor's. She looked surprised at his lighthearted exchange with the lodge's cook and head housekeeper.

Gerald spoke up. "Everyone at the main lodge okay, Millie?"

The older woman chuckled as she began slicing into the chocolate-frosted cake. "They cleaned their plates, if that's any way to judge."

Taylor accepted a thick slice. "For some reason, I thought everyone would be staying in the same building."

"It used to be that way," Gerald replied. "But I found some years back that I liked my privacy. So I moved into this cabin. Seth and Josh have their own place over in the next clearing. There are three other cabins for hunters and fishermen and two more for the hired help, in addition to the rooms at the lodge."

Millie added, "I stay up at the lodge so I can cater to our guests' every whim. Or at least that's what it says on the brochures we mail out."

Seth laughed. "It must work, Millie. Folks keep coming back."

"For her good cooking," Gerald said and turned back to Taylor. "Most times, Seth and Josh and I eat up at the lodge, but sometimes we have family meals down here. Usually on special occasions. Like tonight.''

Family. Seth wondered if Taylor caught how easily Gerald referred to him and Josh as family. If it bothered her, she didn't betray her emotions.

She patted her grandfather's hand. "This is a special occasion.''

"Yes, but I don't need any cake." Gerald waved away the plate that Millie proffered.

"Oh, now," she admonished, "you're as thin as a ghost. A bit of cake won't hurt you. Even Dr. Wright won't quibble about that.''

"Doctor?" Taylor echoed.

Gerald was the first to fill the awkward pause. "My general M.D. Always after me about fats and cholesterol.''

"He won't mind a slice of cake on your granddaughter's first evening here," Millie insisted, and rather than continue arguing, Gerald accepted.

Yet Seth noticed the man ate only half the slice, just as he had pushed the food around on his plate at dinner. And perhaps it was the flickering firelight, but it seemed the lines on his face were carved deeper than usual this evening. Seth noticed Taylor studying her grandfather. Did she see how frail he was? He hoped she would see and understand. Most of all, he hoped she wouldn't end up disappointing Gerald the way Holly had. The man just wasn't strong enough to take it.

The thought of this gentle, good man being hurt sent Seth to his feet again. "Delicious cake," he told Millie, as he headed for the door. "But I'm going to get on the radio and see what's happened to Josh. He was supposed to come straight home after taking the plane in with that last load of cruise-ship passengers."

Millie laughed. "I'll lay you ten to one Josh took one look at Allison's pretty face and decided he couldn't possibly do just as his father asked."

Seth grunted. "The boy spends entirely too much time looking at pretty faces these days."

"Oh, yes," Millie said, her blue eyes twinkling. "Such odd behavior for a boy sixteen."

Giving no reply, Seth stepped out onto the cabin's porch. Millie followed him, saying she had to get back up to the lodge to check on their guests. But instead of following her up the path, Seth leaned against the wooden porch railing and watched her sturdy, aproned figure disappear among the trees. He didn't really need to get on the radio to know where Josh was. The boy was fascinated by the dual lures of Juneau and females. And though Seth could remember the time when he was just as drawn to the fair sex, he didn't know of anything in Juneau that was half as interesting as the scene spread before him now.

The rain had stopped, but moisture dripped from the leaves of trees and from the cabin's rustic tin roof. Fog rose from the river and threaded among the trees like so many restless specters. It was evening, well after nine o'clock, but the Alaskan June skies had dimmed only slightly. The smell of wood smoke and grilled salmon hung in the air. The faint laughter of guests trickled down from the lodge. Only the buzz of a plane's engine disturbed the serenity.

Seth watched the plane make an expert landing on the river and felt his usual stirring of pride. The boy was a good pilot—never reckless, always in control. Until this year, those same qualities could have been applied to Josh in all areas of his life. And now...now Seth found himself lecturing his son all the time. Even though Millie and Gerald had both urged him to cut the boy some slack, Seth didn't seem able to do so. He wished his relationship with his son could be as simple as it had once been. Most of all, he wished to protect Josh from some of the mistakes he had made at the same time.

Only a few minutes passed between the landing of the plane and the sound of Josh running up the path from the river. When he reached the steps to Gerald's cabin, Seth cleared his throat.

Like a startled deer, Josh bounded to a halt before coming up onto the porch. "Dad...I didn't see you."

"Didn't think much about me, either, did you?"

Hands shoved in the pockets of his faded jeans, the boy met Seth's gaze straight on. That was one thing Seth gave him credit for—Josh rarely humbled himself. Maybe it would be better if he did. With the growing and filling-out spurt Josh had gone through this winter, he was almost as tall as Seth. It would be easier to discipline a boy this size if he would at least look a little contrite once in a while.

"Well?" Seth prompted. "How come you missed dinner? You know Gerald was counting on you being here to meet his granddaughter. Millie made a special meal."

"I know, sir, and I'm sorry. I didn't want to let Gerald down." Josh pushed a hand through his shaggy dark brown hair and drew a deep breath. "I guess I just lost track of time."

"That excuse is getting ragged around the edges."

"Yes, sir."

For a few moments, father and son shared a long look.

Finally Seth jerked his head toward the cabin. "Well, get inside. Millie saved you dinner—"

"That's okay, I already—"

Seth narrowed his eyes.

"—ate," Josh finished lamely.

Seth felt the beginning of a familiar anger. "You didn't just run out of time, did you? You deliberately did what I asked you not to do."

"It wasn't deliberate," Josh protested. "That group I took in just wanted me to have a burger with them at the Red Dog."

"You could have said no."

The boy had no answer for that logic.

Seth studied him for a minute. "You're too young to be hanging around the Red Dog Saloon."

"All I had was a burger and some pop."

"That's not the point."

Tone sharpening, Josh fell back on his favorite lament, "Dad, come on. I'm not a little kid."

"Then don't act like one."

Behind Seth a door opened, and he turned to find Taylor framed in the light from within. Her gaze darted between man and boy and she hesitated in the doorway. "I'm sorry, I didn't mean to interrupt. But Grandfather was tired and I insisted he go to bed, and I was just—"

"No problem," Seth cut in smoothly. "Come out and meet my son."

She stepped forward, closing the door behind her, and Josh came up the steps, his brown eyes fairly popping out of his head.

"You're Gerald's granddaughter?" the boy said, ignoring the hand she stretched out to him.

Taylor smiled. "You sound surprised."

"I thought you'd be old."

Exasperated, Seth murmured, "Where are your manners?" while Taylor's delighted laughter rippled through the still evening air.

"I'm sorry," Josh stammered, belatedly pumping her hand in greeting. "It's just that you're not...I mean, you're so..."

Taylor only laughed again, smoothing over the boy's embarrassment. And it was with distinct masculine approval that Josh's gaze swept up the snug blue jean skirt and fitted white blouse, which she had changed into for dinner.

The approval sent a trickle of alarm through Seth. Only hours ago, he had caught this woman's body close to his own and felt a similar, male response. Even though he knew he had to face the fact that his son was growing up, it seemed odd to think of both of them being attracted to the same woman. It was more than odd. It was downright uncomfortable, and he just wouldn't have it.

"Son," he said, in a tone harsher than he had intended. "I think you've got a few things to do before you get to bed. It's getting late."

Josh stared at him, slack-jawed, dull color staining his fine, high cheekbones. "Dad..."

"Don't argue with me, Josh."

"But, Dad—"

"I'll see you tomorrow," Taylor interjected.

The boy's chest swelled visibly under her smile. Without a backward glance at his father, he took the stairs two at a time and jogged toward the lodge.

When Seth turned back to Taylor, she was frowning. He could sense her disapproval and steeled himself for a lecture on how to treat a teenager. It seemed to him that everyone who didn't have a child was all too eager to offer advice on discipline and father-son relationships.

But it wasn't Josh who was on Taylor's mind. "I need to know something from you."

He waited while she took a deep breath.

"Tell me," she whispered finally. "Is my grandfather dying?"

Chapter Two

"... Sometimes I think that if Mother hadn't died, if she hadn't left us alone together, then Dad wouldn't have been so hard on me. I wish Mother were here. I'm sure she would understand how I feel...."

The words in her mother's diary echoed Taylor's sentiments as she stood in a clearing near the lodge. Overhead, the trees swayed in the slight breeze. Morning sunlight, welcome after the rain and gloom of yesterday, warmed the air. Yet Taylor shivered as she closed the diary and gazed at a carved headstone. Sarah Taylor Austin, Beloved Wife and Mother was the inscription. This was her grandmother's grave.

Taylor had always known she was named for her grandmother, but she knew little else about her. Yesterday, Gerald had told her that Sarah had died in childbirth. A slender concrete cross marked the grave of the baby, a boy, who had followed her in death. This child, ten years younger than Holly, would have been Taylor's uncle.

So much sadness. So much death. Taylor sighed. Perhaps it was inevitable that Holly and Gerald had parted with such bitterness.

Yet once upon a time there must have been happiness in their home. Last night before dinner, Taylor and Gerald had looked through an old photo album. Most of the pictures were faded, many of them dog-eared from too much handling. There were lots of pictures of Gerald and Sarah, the two of them bursting with newly married pride as they carved out a place for themselves in this last American wilderness. Through the album, Taylor had followed her mother's growth from a chubby-cheeked baby to a slender teenager. And after Holly disappeared from the pictures, she had seen Gerald grow gaunter, sterner. At least until Josh and Seth started showing up in the photographs. Then the smile Taylor had glimpsed in the earlier snapshots had returned to Gerald's face.

She glanced back toward the lodge, where Gerald was still at breakfast with the guests. A two-storied structure, built of stone and wood, the lodge had fulfilled all her romantic notions. And her grandfather was exactly the sort of man she had dreamed he would be.

When Taylor had slipped out for a walk a little while ago, he had been regaling all those assembled with stories about his early years in this valley. He was droll and witty, thoroughly entertaining, and Taylor had enjoyed listening to him. But she needed a few minutes alone to sort out her thoughts. Her wanderings had brought her to this quiet spot.

She slipped the diary into the pocket of her Windbreaker and took a seat on a nearby tree stump, turning her face up toward the sun. Yet still the warmth didn't reach her bones. Ever since last night, she had been cold, chilled with foreboding.

Her grandfather was ill. His color was bad, and just the short walk from their cabin to the lodge had left him gasping for breath this morning. He had dismissed her concern with an airy wave of his hand and a story about Holly as a child. Taylor had tried to question Millie about Gerald, but the woman had been too busy with breakfast preparations to talk. And Seth Hardy—well, it was obvious he was never going to share any information with her.

Seth Hardy. The name soured in Taylor's mind as she recalled the conversation they'd had out on the porch last night. Not only had Seth sidestepped her questions about Gerald's health, but he had somehow managed to bring the conversation back to his ridiculous assumption that she had come for some inheritance.

After she had asked if Gerald was dying, Seth had stood for a long moment, staring at her, apparently nonplussed by her blunt question.

"I didn't mean to ask in quite that way," she amended, careful to keep her voice low so she wouldn't wake Gerald. "But it's obvious that he isn't well."

Seth's gaze slipped from hers as he leaned against a wooden porch post and looked toward the river. "He's not a young man anymore."

"But sixty-eight isn't old these days, either, so why—"

"He had a nasty bout with pneumonia this winter. It left him weak."

"Why isn't he in a hospital?"

"His doctor released him."

Taylor snorted. "Then he needs another doctor."

"What he doesn't need is your interference."

The man's low, threatening tone made Taylor stiffen. "Why yours and not mine?"

"Because I'm the only family he's known for nearly sixteen years."

There was no doubt the two men were close. In fact, the Seth Hardy who talked with Gerald and joked with Millie bore little resemblance to the distrustful, taciturn individual she had dealt with thus far. But perhaps he was too close to Gerald to see what to her were the obvious signs of a serious illness.

She placed a hand on Seth's arm, forcing him to turn toward her again. For her grandfather's sake, she didn't want to fight with this man. "I know you don't like me. I know you have the misguided notion that my reasons for being here are less than aboveboard."

"Why are you here?"

"I want to know my grandfather. He's the only blood relation I have in all the world."

"And why is that *suddenly* so important?"

The accumulated weariness of weeks of anticipation and two days of traveling claimed Taylor as she considered Seth's pointed question. Her shoulders sagged. Why was this so important, anyway?

For most of her life, she hadn't cared that she had a grandfather living somewhere in Alaska. If she had, she would have pressed her mother for details long ago. All that had changed the moment she read her mother's diary. Gerald had become something more than a nebulous idea. He had sprung to life on those pages. It had been easy for Taylor to read between the lines of Holly's teenage anger and see what had really happened all those years ago. She had realized he wasn't the uncompromising monster Holly had said he was. And now... now that Taylor had seen him, had looked into his eyes and felt the warmth of his smile, she knew she wanted to know him. She wanted more than faded photographs by which to remember Gerald Austin.

Rather feebly, she had tried to explain her feelings to Seth. "He's my grandfather. I want to make up for lost time."

"Oh, really." A world of doubt was registered in Seth's two drawled words.

And once again, he angered Taylor. "No matter what you think of me, I have a right to know what's wrong with *my* grandfather."

Fury, raw and unchecked, twisted his even features. He grasped Taylor's shoulders, his hard fingers digging into her flesh, holding her steady even though she tried to shrug off his touch. "Don't talk to me about *your* rights," he muttered.

"But he's my—"

"Until a few weeks ago, Gerald was nothing to you."

"But that's changed."

"That remains to be seen." He released Taylor so abruptly that she stumbled backward as he started down the steps.

Infuriated by his manner, she hissed after him, "What gives you the right to treat me this way?"

On the bottom step, Seth wheeled around to face her. "Gerald's my friend and more of a father than the man who sired me ever was. He and Josh and I have a history together. That gives me more rights than you or that sainted mother of yours—"

"Don't talk about my mother," Taylor cut in, jumping at the sarcasm in his tone. "You don't know anything about her."

"I know more than you think." And with those words, he turned and disappeared through the fog that danced among the trees.

Taylor had stared after him, shaking with fury.

That anger seized her again as she sat in the morning sun beside her grandmother's grave. Seth Hardy was arrogant, cold and nasty.

And Gerald considered him a member of the family.

But what would Gerald say if Taylor told him how Seth had treated her? She considered that notion for only a second. For she couldn't tell Gerald about Seth. Gerald would just be upset. It would probably seem as if Taylor were trying to drive a wedge between the two men. She would look like the schemer Seth thought she was. No, it was better to handle Seth and his misguided notions about her on her own.

Groaning, Taylor dropped her chin onto her cupped hands. She was wishing Seth Hardy didn't exist when a twig snapped in the forest behind her. She whirled around. The object of her fury stood at the edge of the clearing.

He walked toward her, long, denim-clad legs carrying him forward in a deceptively lazy stroll. The laziness didn't fool Taylor. Seth reminded her of a wolf, stalking his prey.

Only she wasn't about to be stalked. She stood and faced him.

"You might want to be careful about wandering around," he said, coming to a stop in front of her. "We have some bears who hang around the lodge. They're kind of used to us, but they're still dangerous if you don't know how to deal with them." His grin was slight. "Especially if they're hungry."

Taylor glanced around at the surrounding woods, certain he was putting her on. "It's hard to believe wild animals would come this close."

"Oh, we get bears, foxes, mountain goats, moose, to name just a few. There's really no cause for alarm. You just need to be aware."

"Well, thank you," Taylor said stiffly. "I appreciate your making me aware. But now if you'll excuse me..." She turned and started to leave, not anxious to spend any more time than necessary in this man's company.

"Taylor..."

The humble note in his voice took her by surprise. She stopped and faced him again.

Hands on his lean hips, he cleared his throat, looked at her and then looked away.

"Well?"

"About last night..." He stopped, shook his head, then fastened his gaze on her again. "Maybe I was out of line," he said, sounding as if the admission cost him a great effort.

Taylor tilted her chin upward, half pleased, half irritated by his reluctant apology. "Maybe?"

His eyes narrowed. "I got angry. I shouldn't have."

"So you're sorry about being angry, but not sorry about what you said."

Seth had to swallow a sharp retort. He was determined not to argue with Taylor. Last night while he lay awake, turning their conversation round in his mind, he realized he had made a mistake in being so openly antagonistic. It would have been much better to cultivate her friendship. She would reveal her true colors much sooner to someone she trusted.

"I'm sorry about it all," he said now, through gritted teeth.

She laughed, a vibrant sound that echoed through the trees, but the humor didn't quite reach her eyes. "You don't sound sorry, Mr. Hardy."

"Well, I am," he retorted. "And you can drop the Mister business."

"All right, *Seth*." She took another step forward. "I hope you are sorry, because I am. I'm sorry we got off on the wrong foot. I can see you care for my grandfather, and whether you choose to believe me or not, I do, too."

Seth kept his skepticism to himself. "It means a lot to Gerald that you're here."

She looked at him for a few moments, leaving Seth with the definite feeling that she distrusted him as much as he did her. "For Gerald's sake, I think we should try to get along, even if that means just staying out of each other's way."

He was planning to watch her every move, but she didn't need to know that. "All right."

"Good." Taylor stuck out her hand.

Seth studied that small but capable-looking hand for a moment before taking it in his own. Her skin was as soft as he remembered from yesterday when he had tried to help her into the plane. He could also remember how she had felt in his arms—slender but with definite, yielding curves. He tried not to think about that sensation as he looked into her hazel eyes. Nothing muddied a man's reasoning like sexual attraction. He wasn't, couldn't be attracted to her.

Yet it was Taylor who pulled her hand away first.

Pink tinged her cheeks as she backed away. "I'm going to the lodge to find Gerald."

Still thinking of the softness of her skin, Seth stuck his hands into his jeans pockets and nodded. "See you later."

As she hurried away, Seth did his best not to notice the sway of her hips or the way the sunshine picked up the gold in her hair.

Muttering an oath, he left the clearing. He had better things to do them admire a woman's looks. One of the outboard motors needed repairs. The Juneau office should be called to see how many cruise passengers were scheduled for dinner. A mountain of paperwork also waited on his desk.

But somehow, his usual daily tasks seemed even more mundane when compared with the thought of Taylor Cantrell's gently rounded fanny.

"Lord help us," he growled as he headed for the boat house. "I'm acting as randy as Josh."

However, no amount of self-reproach kept his gaze from dwelling on Taylor's pretty features after lunch in the lodge. Seated at one of the dining hall's tables, she was surrounded by admiring males—two guests on either side and Josh hanging over her shoulder as they studied a map of the area. There was no reason for the sudden clenching in Seth's gut. At least no logical reason. But the feeling intensified as Taylor's laughter, a musical, sweet sound, reached him.

A touch on his shoulder made him jerk around.

Gerald's bristling white eyebrows lifted in surprise as he took the seat beside Seth. "Didn't mean to startle you."

"I guess I was lost in thought."

"No problems, I hope." His gaze moving toward Taylor, Gerald smiled. "I don't think I'm going to be much use to you this summer, Seth. I just want to spend my time with her."

Taylor wasn't the only reason Gerald wouldn't be participating much in the tourist rush, but that didn't bear discussion now. So Seth nodded. "I hope it'll be a good summer."

"Me, too." Gerald frowned then, glancing back at Seth. "I'd appreciate it if you'd show her around, take her to some of my favorite spots."

"Me?" Seth said, startled. "But you—"

"I won't be going many places," the older man murmured. "You and I both know that."

Knowing it and talking about it were two separate matters. An unexpected swell of emotion forced Seth to clear his throat. "Oh, now," he said, his voice deliberately careless, "in a few weeks you'll probably be taking the floatplane into Juneau everyday."

Gerald's smile couldn't quite mask his sadness.

"You two look like conspirators."

Taylor's voice, so happy and full of life, sent resentment crackling through Seth. She had left her admirers across the room and was now at Gerald's side, putting a hand on his shoulder, smiling down at him. How could she laugh, Seth wondered, glaring at her. Couldn't she see? Didn't she care?

Muttering an apology, he got up and stalked away.

Puzzled, Taylor watched him leave the room and spoke before she thought. "I don't believe your partner likes me."

"Oh, it just takes a while to get to know Seth. It's worth the effort, though."

She was skeptical. "Is it?"

"He's a fine man. A hard worker, and a good father. He'd do anything for Josh."

"They were arguing last night," Taylor murmured, remembering the scene she had interrupted on the porch. She had heard the last part of it.

"All parents and children argue sometimes."

"Seth was talking to Josh as if he were a kid. And he's not."

Gerald sighed. "But that's hard for a parent to realize, Taylor. I made the same mistake with your mother. To my everlasting regret, I made that mistake."

The pain in his voice twisted through Taylor. She sat down beside him, her fingers resting lightly on his thin, blue-veined hand. "Don't think about that."

"There isn't a day that's passed since she left that I haven't thought about it, wished I had handled things differently." He looked at Taylor. "I never thought she'd run away. No matter what, I didn't believe she would leave me, leave her home."

"She thought she was in love," Taylor murmured. "It's all in the diary. She was so confused—"

"And I was too busy to see how serious it was. Too busy and too blind. I wish Seth would learn from my mistakes."

"Seth?" Taylor looked up, following Gerald's gaze to the doorway where Seth had reappeared and stood talking with Josh. Father and son looked so similar, tall and straight, square-jawed and male. The chief difference between them was their eyes. Josh's were big and deep brown, soulful, reflecting his every feeling. Unlike his father, he was not yet cynical and cold.

But he would be, she decided as the two of them turned to go. Even across the room she could sense Josh's anger. He reminded her of a match, smoldering, almost ready to flame. Perhaps all teenagers were that way. She could remember some passionate outbursts, herself. She already liked Josh and would like to help him if she could.

To Gerald, she said, "Maybe Josh has too many responsibilities for someone his age."

Gerald shook his head. "It isn't the work that bothers Josh. He has always been willing to help, especially when he gets to fly. Airplanes were his first love. He got that much from his father."

"Well, he's not happy. That much is pretty clear."

"And the problem is mainly what we just said—Seth still sees Josh as a child. It's not hard to do. Sometimes I still think of him as that lost, little sad-eyed boy Seth brought to the lodge one summer."

"Where was his mother?"

"She decided she couldn't raise the boy."

"You never knew her?"

"The marriage was a brief one, and it was over before Seth came north."

"How old was Josh?"

"He was just three when Seth brought him here." Gerald grinned. "He was such a little fella, scared as all get out, but trying hard not to show it. Of course, Millie was crazy about him from the start." He paused. "We all were."

"And he hasn't seen his mother since?" Taylor asked, feeling an even stronger kinship with the boy.

Gerald settled back in his chair, a troubled look on his face. "I don't believe Seth has encouraged any curiosity about her. A mistake, I think."

"Definitely."

There was a pause, then, "Do you regret not knowing your father, Taylor?"

"I have Joe," she replied, not even pausing to think. "He's the best father in the world. I don't think my biological father could have compared. I know you didn't like him."

Gerald's frown deepened. "Maybe he wasn't such a bad sort. Just too old for Holly, too experienced, too... too much, I guess."

Taylor patted his hands again. "You would like Joe. He made Mom very happy. She was always laughing. We all took care of each other."

"That's good," Gerald whispered, his gnarled fingers gripping hers with surprising strength. "Joe will always have my gratitude for putting you and me together."

She grinned. "Not all stepmothers or stepfathers are wicked. Josh would have probably been better off if Seth had remarried."

"A good point," Gerald conceded. "But I'm afraid Seth's experiences soured him on women. With the exception of Millie, of course."

"But yesterday, Allison said he makes women swoon."

A slight smile crooked the corners of Gerald's mouth. "I do believe Seth enjoys a certain reputation with the ladies. It isn't the sort that leads to marriage."

Taylor laughed at his delicate choice of words. "The love 'em and leave 'em sort?"

"But the right woman could settle him down."

"I don't know. Those types of men rarely change."

"I did."

"Don't tell me you were a heartbreaker, too."

"In my day, yes. Then along came your grand-mother...." He put a hand to his heart, a merry twinkle in his eyes. "And I was a goner."

Delighted by this romantic streak in him, Taylor crossed her arms on the table and leaned forward. "Is that why you never remarried?"

"There was no one like my Sarah," he proclaimed. His gaze traveled around the now-empty room. "She and I built this place with our own hands. We started with this room right here and kept adding on till the lodge was just as you see it. We used all her money."

"Her money?"

"She had inherited a little from her father, a lot more than the nest egg I had saved up before we married. We invested all of it in this place. And she worked beside me, day and night, to get the hunting and fishing operation started. Long before tourists were streaming up this way, your grandmother knew they would come. She and I had a dream of sharing this beautiful land with others. I wish she could see it now."

He sighed, and sadness once more chased the merriment from his face. "Sarah was my love. But I should have remarried. For your mother's sake. Holly would have been better off...." His voice trailing away, he shook his head.

Taylor realized then that no matter how she steered the conversation, her grandfather always came back to his regrets over Holly. She wished she could erase some of his sadness. The regrets she knew he would have forever, but perhaps she could keep him smiling.

Standing, she held out her hand. "Come on, let's go back to the cabin. I want to show you some of my work. I brought some of Mom's paintings, too. She was really very good."

Though there was eagerness in his gaze, he hesitated. "Sure you want to spend the afternoon with me? It's rare that we have this much sunshine. I think Josh or someone else is going to lead a hike up one of the mountains."

"I've got weeks and weeks to explore the mountains." Taylor slipped her hand in his. "I'd rather spend the day with you."

"Then let's go."

From a window in the lodge kitchen, Seth watched Taylor and Gerald walk toward their cabin. They were arm in arm, the man's thin shoulders held high, a lightness in his step that Seth hadn't seen in some time.

"It will be okay."

Glancing at Millie, who had joined him beside the window, Seth shrugged. "I hope so."

"Taylor's not what we were afraid she'd be."

"Maybe not." To Seth's surprise, he wanted to believe Millie was right.

As Taylor and Gerald disappeared from view, the older woman sighed. "I think he should tell her the truth."

Seth turned from the window. At the other end of the room, two of the college coeds hired for the summer were talking as they loaded a dishwasher. They weren't interested in Seth and Millie's conversation, yet he still dropped his voice. "Gerald won't tell her. You know that."

"Then we should."

"We promised we wouldn't, remember?"

Millie's pink bow of a mouth thinned. "I wasn't thinking when I made that promise. I don't know how he got me to do it."

Seth grinned. "He's always been pretty good at wrapping us all around his finger."

Millie sniffed, but before she could reply, Josh banged through the back door, hefting several institutional-size cans of tomatoes. One of the kitchen helpers, a pretty brunette at least three years Josh's senior, flashed him a bright smile. Josh grinned back.

Stiffening, Seth watched the exchange through narrowed eyes. But before he could send Josh about his business, Millie's light touch on his arm stopped him.

She bustled forward. "Josh, put those cans on the counter. I'm making chili this afternoon. Not everyone wants grilled salmon three meals a day."

Still grinning at the brunette, Josh put the cans down. "Anything else I can do to help out in here?"

"You? Help in my kitchen?" Millie asked, pretending to be horrified. "You'd destroy all the utensils, rearrange my cabinets and probably devour all the food yourself."

The two kitchen helpers giggled, Josh teased Millie again and Seth looked down at the clipboard he held, trying not to listen. But the supply list Millie had given him was no match for the young, lighthearted voices. They sounded happy and carefree. Taylor had sounded the same way after lunch today. Had Seth ever been as young, ever laughed with such untroubled abandon?

Of course he had. Sometime, long ago. And recently, too. His life was good, every moment filled. He knew the satisfaction of working hard and seeing his business grow. He had the camaraderie of the pilots and people who worked for the lodge each summer. He had Millie's friendship. He had Gerald. And most importantly, he had Josh.

Seth glanced up, studying the face of the young man across the room. Where had the little boy gone? If he could just remember the moment when the boy had changed into a man, then perhaps he could deal with the resulting change in their relationship. The change had come so quickly. Its effect was so profound. If they stepped back for just a while, could they recapture some of their old ease? It was worth a try, at least.

"Hey, Josh," Seth said, having to raise his voice over the girls' laughter.

The boy straightened from the counter. "Sir?"

"How about you and me taking off for some fishing?"

"Fishing?" Josh's surprise was evident. "But it's the middle of the week. We've got guests and stuff."

"I feel like fishing."

Still, his son looked dumbfounded. "I thought since it wasn't raining for once, that I was supposed to put a coat of paint on the dock house."

"The weather looks like it'll hold. You could paint later."

Josh shifted from foot to foot. "Well...uh...I was hoping I could take the tourists into Juneau again."

Disappointment roughened Seth's response. "After last night?"

"I promise to be home early. Allison asked me to have dinner with her folks. And I could pick up Millie's supplies, too."

Seth started to refuse. He wanted to order Josh to stay here, to spend the afternoon with him. Yet what would that accomplish, other than to drive still another wedge between them? So he shrugged, tore the list of supplies off the clipboard and handed it to Josh. "Suit yourself, son. We'll fish another day."

"Sure." The boy took the list, his dark eyes shining. He pushed open the door, disappeared for a moment, then popped back inside. "Hey, Dad...thanks, okay?"

"Sure," Seth said, trying to sound as offhand as the boy. And in a moment, Josh's whoop of joy could be heard as he ran down the trail behind the lodge.

Looking up, Seth found Millie regarding him with a sympathetic gaze. With barely a nod in her direction, he stomped out of the kitchen and through the lodge. He didn't need the woman's pity. So his son would rather spend an evening with a girl than an afternoon with his nearly forty-year-old dad. Nothing strange about that. Seth was crazy to be so disappointed. One fishing trip wasn't going to make things the way they had been between him and his son.

He and Josh had changed for good.

Everything was changing.

And Seth's whole life was tilting in an unknown direction.

Since he had become Gerald's partner and brought Josh to live here, Seth had a focus for his life. Josh and Gerald—they had centered him, calmed him. Now those two people were slipping away. He was losing them both.

Seth had faced losses before. As a child in a loveless home. In a plane over a jungle battlefield. With a woman who discarded him like some worn-out piece of clothing. Yet he had always survived.

But this time... oh, this time. He was damned if he knew how he would survive these changes.

Chapter Three

"He noticed me today. He looked right at me and smiled. I couldn't breathe. And I couldn't stop looking back...."

High above the river, a bald eagle soared. The black-brown feathers and snow-white head made a bold statement against the gloomy, dark clouds. Pencil flying across her sketch pad, Taylor tried in vain to capture the creature's innate majesty. The graceful wings spanned six feet or more. The broad tail spread wide as the bird spiraled low along the shore, and the razor-sharp talons reached to claim a fat salmon that had died and washed up on the rocks. The reality of the bird was more elusive and more powerful than any lines on any paper could ever express.

Taylor sighed in frustration. During her first week at the lodge, she had tried many times to sketch this bird and others like it, but she just couldn't get it right. "It's like chasing shadows," she murmured.

Seated beside her on a broad, flat rock, Josh protested, "No, no you've got him this time. You've really got him."

Above them, the eagle circled, then came to rest in his wide nest at the top of a tree. According to Gerald, the moss-lined nest was many years old. He claimed to have made more than a passing acquaintance with the progression of eagles who had made this spot their home. Indeed, the first time Taylor visited the nest with her grandfather, she thought the resident eagle had inclined his head just slightly in greeting. Today, she and Josh merited nary a glance.

Frowning down at her rough drawing, she tried shading in some details, then gave up in disgust. She started to rip out the page, but Josh stopped her.

"Can I have it?"

"It isn't any good."

"I say it is."

"Okay." With a flourish, she tore the sheet out and presented it to the teenager. "With my compliments."

"Sign it first."

"I'm not sure I want to claim it," she said, but she scrawled her name across the bottom just the same.

Josh's brown eyes shown. "Someday this will be valuable—an original Taylor Cantrell sketch."

"Yeah, a Taylor Cantrell and a dollar might get you a can of pop in Chicago."

"I'll remember that when I make it to Chicago."

The two of them laughed easily together, but Taylor didn't miss how Josh looked at the sketch. And at her. His admiration for her was very touching. But she made no special concessions to Josh. Perhaps that was why he responded to her, why he liked her company. She just treated him like a friend, an equal. In the past week, they had spent quite a few hours together, walking in the woods, talking together or with Gerald. Josh was full of typical teenage angst, but on the whole, Taylor found him easy to be with, fun and really quite undemanding.

Not at all like his father.

Now why did I have to think of him? she asked herself in irritation. Since declaring their truce last week, she and Seth Hardy had managed to stay out of each other's way. At least there had been no overt contact, no more heated words, no accusations, no rebuttals. Yet she always knew he was there. Waiting. Watching. What was it that he expected her to do, anyway?

More importantly, why did she spend so much time worrying about him? He was nothing to her. Thoughts of him shouldn't have claimed so much of her attention.

She didn't realize she was frowning until Josh said, "Something wrong?"

She summoned a smile for him. "I was just wishing everyone was as easy to get along with as you are."

He stretched his long legs, letting his feet dangle over the edge of the rock. "You're talking about Dad, aren't you?"

A perceptive boy, Taylor thought. Or perhaps his father had said something to him about her. "Why do you think your father and I don't get along?"

"Oh, it's not your fault. He can be a real jerk sometimes."

"A jerk?" Though Taylor thought the description was rather apt, she wasn't going to encourage Josh to talk that way about Seth. "That's not a very respectful way to talk about your father, is it?"

His jaw set in a square line not unlike that of the man he was criticizing. "Maybe it isn't, but I've noticed the way he treats you."

"He doesn't *treat* me at all. We don't have much to say to each other. That's no crime."

"No, it's just Dad acting like a jerk."

"Josh—"

He interrupted before she could give him another gentle rebuke. "Tell me about Chicago."

The city she knew and loved the best was definitely a more interesting topic than Josh's father. Setting her sketch pad aside, Taylor drew her legs up and hugged her knees close to her chest. "What do you want to know?"

"How does it sound?"

That puzzled her. "How does the city sound?"

"Yeah. Sometimes it's so quiet around here. I feel like I'm going to lose my mind."

Taylor cocked her head, listening to the rustle of wind in the trees, the calls of a bird far up in the forest, the gentle lap of the water against the rocky shore. Funny, she hadn't noticed the quiet. Even though she had always professed to love the hustle and bustle of city streets, she hadn't once missed the noise.

Josh pillowed his hands under his head, and his voice took on a dreamy quality. "I bet it's never quiet in Chicago."

She shook her head. "For the most part it's pretty loud. Horns blaring. People talking, arguing. Music playing—"

"It sounds like your drawings look."

"My drawings?"

"The ones you brought to show Gerald. He showed them to me and Dad last night while you were helping Millie after dinner."

The thought of Seth thumbing through her work hit Taylor in a most disturbing way. At Gerald's request, she had brought some of her best work to show him. Most of the pieces were cityscapes, impressionistic urban studies in black and charcoal with flashes of color denoting the energy of the people who made the city work. She couldn't imagine Seth liking them, for she couldn't imagine him at home in any setting but this. He would be lost among the concrete and glass towers.

Fervently, Josh said, "I'd like to hear the city. Someday I will."

"If you really want, there's no place you can't visit." Taylor gestured to their surroundings. "But I warn you, it's a world away from this."

"Good. I can't wait to leave this."

She smiled at his impatience. Kids never changed, she guessed. She could remember how much she had wanted to leave home and have her own place. College had brought her the opportunity she craved, but barely two weeks passed before she had scurried home for reassurance and a home-cooked dinner. And after graduation, when she really moved out, she recalled standing in her old bedroom, knowing it was just the same as she had left it, but aware that it would never be fully hers again, either.

Those memories weren't something she could explain to Josh now. He was too young to understand, too impatient to leave. Maybe she should allow him to read her mother's diary. The words Holly had written just before and after she had left Alaska spoke more eloquently than Taylor ever could about the pain of leaving home.

Like Josh, Holly had wanted to see something other than these mountains and this valley. But she'd had her regrets. In those early years, she had written about wanting to come home. She might well have come home if she hadn't felt the door was locked tight against her. She was mistaken, that much Taylor was sure of now that she had met Gerald, but Holly hadn't

felt she had any options but to stay away. Words—
bitter, angry words had kept her away.

Taylor glanced toward the snow-capped peaks in the
distance. How many times had her mother wished to
see her mountains again? Had she stood in this spot,
beneath the eagle's nest and dreamed of faraway
places? Closing her eyes, imagining her mother here,
Taylor could almost feel her presence. The sensation
warmed her, pleased her.

"Hello, you two."

Gerald's voice broke the spell, but Taylor opened
her eyes to greet him with a smile. The smile slipped
only a little when she saw he was accompanied by
Seth. She told herself she should be grateful Seth was
there. Gerald seemed to falter a little each day. He
didn't need to be wandering around by himself. In
fact, he looked as if he shouldn't be wandering at all,
but resting in his cabin. Rest was something he never
seemed to do, however. She had awakened many times
during the past few nights and heard him knocking
about the cabin. He wouldn't talk to her about it,
however. Seth, of course, was unapproachable on the
subject. And Millie just set her mouth when Taylor
tried to talk to her. Taylor didn't know what else to do.

She tried to keep the worry out of her face as the
two men approached the rock. Her voice deliberately
light, she said, "Josh and I were discussing Chicago."

Gerald's smile was slight. "It's not a bad place, as
big cities go."

"You were there?" Taylor asked, surprised.

Gerald seemed to hesitate before answering. "Yes, I paid Chicago a visit."

"Before you moved here?"

His answer was an evasive, "Long, long ago."

"Maybe Chicago's where I'll go to college," Seth cut in, a defiant gleam in his eye.

If the statement was an attempt to get a rise out of his father, Seth didn't take the bait. His expression as unreadable as usual, he braced one foot on the rock's side and stood as if surveying the surroundings. "I'll put this view right here up against anything any city in the world has to offer."

"I didn't realize you were so widely traveled," Taylor drawled, wanting to provoke the man, yet not sure of why.

His flinty gray-eyed gaze met hers straight on. "Tokyo, Honolulu, New York, San Francisco, Saigon, London—I'd say I've had a fair sample of what the world has to offer."

In answer, Taylor merely raised an eyebrow.

Josh was still insistent. "Well, I think I'd like Chicago. At least if it's anything like Taylor's drawings of Chicago."

Again, Taylor's gaze flashed to Seth's. He nodded. "You do have a way of capturing a city's grit."

She wasn't sure whether she had been complimented or accused.

Hands in his pockets, Gerald cocked his head back to study the eagle's nest. "I'd like to see Taylor apply some of her talent to this place."

"She has," Josh said, offering the eagle sketch as proof.

Gerald studied the picture for a few moments. "Well, this settles matters. I want to commission a drawing."

"Oh, Grandfather—"

"No, no," he said. "You're not getting out of this, Taylor. You're a part of the Eagle Lodge family. The space over the mantel in the dining room has been taken up by that deer's head for far too long. It's your duty to replace it. I want a finished drawing of this eagle to commemorate your first summer here at the lodge."

"That'd be cool," Josh agreed.

Gerald turned to Seth. "What do you think?"

"I think it's up to Taylor," he replied smoothly, gray eyes still intent on hers. "From what I saw, her specialty is city streets—maybe there's no challenge for her in painting eagles or mountains."

Taylor's arms tightened around her legs. Seth Hardy needed to understand there was no challenge she wasn't up to.

"She can draw anything," Josh insisted, glaring at his father.

Seth's face flicked from the boy's face, then back to hers. "Josh's confidence alone should inspire you, Taylor."

"It does," she replied with complete sincerity.

Gerald spoke before Seth could. "Then it's settled, Taylor. You'll work on an eagle for the mantel."

"For you, Grandfather, I'll do anything," she promised blithely, even though her words caused furrows to deepen on Seth's brow.

"Come on, Josh," Gerald invited. "Millie wants your help in moving some furniture, and I want you to tell me about that bear you guys spotted on the guests' hike yesterday."

Josh abandoned his sprawled pose on the rock without hesitation. The two of them strode off through the woods, the older man's white hair bent close to the dark head of the teenager who was recounting in vivid detail yesterday's wildlife encounter.

Affection spread through Taylor as she watched them disappear from view. "Josh is so great to him. He really seems to enjoy being with Gerald."

Nodding, Seth pulled himself up on the rock and settled on the spot his son had vacated. Taylor was surprised, but she didn't move away. She didn't want this man to know how uncomfortable his nearness made her. Yet she couldn't ignore his proximity, either. She always reacted to his presence and today was no exception.

In snug jeans and flannel shirt, he was completely, blatantly male. She shouldn't care. She told herself she *didn't* care. But now, as happened whenever Seth was near, she noticed little things about him—like his broad, strong-looking hands or the way his tone lightened when he spoke to Gerald or how one eyelid drooped just a bit lower than the other.

Just like the eagle, she had tried and failed to capture Seth in a sketch. But her interest in him was more than an artist registering the details of a subject. Perhaps it was because she wasn't used to people disliking her. Perhaps it was that he was so different from any other man she had known. But for whatever the reason, he fascinated her.

Deceptively relaxed, he braced his hands behind him and stretched out on the rock. "You're right," he said. "Gerald and Josh are close. When Josh was small and had a cold or didn't feel well, the first person he wanted was Gerald. They would bundle up in a chair by the fire, and Gerald would spin some yarns about hunting bears and getting lost in snowstorms. Soon Josh would forget he was feeling bad."

The expression on Seth's face, a faraway, yearning look, intrigued Taylor. He came across so much of the time as a hard, uncompromising man. Yet here was this glimpse of softness. "Josh is really special. I'm sure you're proud of him."

"He's a good boy," Seth returned in his typical no-nonsense fashion. "Too big for his britches sometimes, but a good boy, nonetheless."

Taylor smiled. Seth sounded as if he were talking about a ten-year-old instead of young man nearly grown. She took a deep breath of the clean, cool air. "Josh will miss this place."

His gaze sharpened. "What do you mean?"

"When Josh goes to college, or off on those travels he talks about all the time, he'll miss this place. He doesn't realize it now, but he will."

"Josh will come back." The words were spoken with quiet authority.

Taylor couldn't resist needling Seth a bit about his confidence. "You sound like a king who is quite sure of his subjects' loyalty."

"That's what Josh told me last night after I said he couldn't spend the night in Juneau. Except he called me a tyrant instead of a king."

"Is he right?" The pointed question slipped out before Taylor considered its wisdom, but she didn't back down. "Do you think you're a tyrant?"

Seth, his posture no longer so relaxed, replied. "If protecting what's mine makes me a tyrant, then so be it."

"What's yours?" she murmured, amused by his possessive tone.

"My family, my business."

"You won't always be able to protect Josh."

"But I can now."

The curtness of his reply told Taylor she was treading on dangerous ground. His relationship with his son really was none of her business, but she kept on. "I'll bet my grandfather thought he could protect my mother, too. But she ran away."

Now Seth sat up, his gaze sharpening further. "Are you trying to say Josh is going to run away?"

"No, of course not," Taylor said quickly. "At least if he is, he hasn't told me anything about it."

"I'm surprised. He's been spending a lot of time with you."

She bristled at the disapproval in his tone. "Maybe he just needs to talk to someone with a different perspective."

Seth looked as if he was about to protest, then apparently reconsidered. "Maybe you're right."

Taylor put a hand to her forehead, adopting a melodramatic tone. "Can this be right? Are you and I actually agreeing on something?" She reached for her sketch pad and pencils. "Excuse me while I mark this down."

And to her surprise, Seth laughed.

The laughter relaxed the stern set of his jaw, took years from his face and forced an answering smile from Taylor. It felt good for once to let down her guard with him. And yet she became all the more aware of his nearness. She was tempted to touch him, to put out her hand and stroke his cheek or the back of his hand. The impulse shocked her, sent color flying to her face.

She tore her gaze from his, searching for something, anything to ease the sudden, odd tension between them. Help came from the river. "Look, one of lodge's boats is coming in with the fishermen. I wonder if it was a good day."

Seth murmured something in reply. He wasn't sure what. He didn't give a damn about how well the salmon were running. He was too busy admiring the flush that left a pink stain on Taylor's cheeks. Her preoccupation with the passing boat gave him an opportunity to study the clean, pure lines of her profile. Tendrils of hair, escaping a black bow at the nape of her neck, blew about her cheeks. She looked as young as Josh. But she wasn't. That was what kept throwing Seth off balance. She looked young, but he had sensed a maturity about her from the beginning. He still didn't trust her, but he knew she was no silly, flighty female. He liked that about her.

Just as he liked the way her eyes tilted up at the corners when she smiled. And the sound of her laughter. And the things she did for a simple pair of worn jeans. She had a way of moving that left a man wondering about the body beneath the clothes.

She turned and caught him wondering about her hidden, feminine mysteries. Of course, she couldn't have known his exact thoughts, but he could tell she was aware of the general direction. Seth knew when a woman was reading his mind. Indeed, a little mental communication could be put to good use at the appropriate moment. But most of the women with whom he had communicated in this manner weren't the granddaughters of his closest friend. They weren't fifteen years his junior. And the ache they caused was merely sexual—the wanting didn't spread all the way through his soul, as it was doing now while he looked at Taylor.

He acknowledged all the reasons why he should turn away.

But he didn't.

Fascinated, he watched the muscles that worked in her neck as she swallowed. "So..." she began. "Do you think they'll bring in any king salmon?"

With some effort, he made himself tear his gaze from her face. He shook his head, feeling as if he were in a fog.

"No?"

Puzzled, he said, "No, what?"

"I asked about king salmon and you shook your head."

He forced a slight laugh. Maybe the last few moments had been his imagination. Maybe nothing had passed between him and Taylor. Maybe he was a lonely man who had gone far too long without the comfort of a woman's body. He should do something about that the next time he was in Juneau. He knew a few females who didn't need flowers and promises. Those women didn't confuse him. But in the past year they hadn't completely erased his ache, either.

Taylor was still regarding him with a slight frown, so he made some comment about king salmon. Then, needing something other than her closeness to occupy his attention, he picked up the sketch pad she had discarded.

"Very nice," he said as he flipped back through the pages. Bits and pieces of the surrounding scenery had been roughed in. There was the eagle's nest, the lodge tucked at the base of the sheltering mountains, a salmon leaping from the water. Even in these unfinished pictures, she had caught the movement, the drama to be found in this valley. He had to acknowledge her talent. "You really are very good."

"Thank you," she said. He thought there was a wariness about her that hadn't been present several minutes ago. But maybe that was his imagination, too.

He flipped another page in the book. The angular lines of Gerald's face stared up at him. "I like this. You caught the way he smiles."

Her reserve began to thaw as she leaned forward, studying the sketch. "You think so? I know the eyes are wrong, but I can't seem to get them right. I could never get my mother's eyes right, either, and it's in the eyes that she really looks like Gerald."

Seth had seen pictures of Holly, and he didn't see any overwhelming resemblance between her and Gerald, around the eyes or elsewhere. Taylor would naturally see her mother in a different light. And admittedly, he wasn't one of Holly Cantrell's biggest fans.

He turned another page in the book and remarked, "Your mother was an artist, too, wasn't she?"

"She played at it. She could have been really good if she had studied or pursued it seriously."

"You're serious, though."

"I work hard at it, if that's what you mean."

"Sell many paintings?"

Her grin was rueful. "No, not yet."

"Then how do you eat?"

"I do a lot of free-lance illustration work for ad agencies, magazines—you name it. I stay pretty busy, actually. And in whatever free time I have, I work on my sketches and paintings."

"I guess it wasn't easy to take the summer off."

She glanced down at her hands. "Actually, it was easy. I needed to get away. I had several well-paying projects during the winter, so I didn't have much time to work on my own. I had been feeling..." Her voice trailed away as she looked out at the river again. She shrugged, smiling ruefully. "Well, let's just say the reality of my mother's death only sunk in in the past few months. I don't know what I thought, but...well, anyway, apart from meeting my grandfather, I wanted to use this time to sort of clear my head. There's a gallery that's interested in doing a show next winter."

Even Seth, with his limited knowledge of the art world, knew a show was an important step. "That sounds good."

"It is." Her smile was pure excitement. "But it would be nice to have all the time I need to get ready for it."

It would be nice if Gerald could bankroll my career.

She didn't say that. She didn't even hint at it. But Seth thought it just the same. The doubts he'd had about Taylor from the beginning returned in full force. Only now there was a difference. Now he didn't want to think the worst of her. He didn't want to believe she was anything other than exactly as she appeared. And not just for Gerald's benefit. For his own.

The thought angered him. He told himself he didn't care who or what she was. She was just another woman, out for whatever she could take. So she had a smile sweet enough to touch a man's soul and a way of looking at you that made you feel as though you were the only person on Earth. It wasn't real. It couldn't be real.

Taylor felt the change in Seth. He withdrew. One minute they were talking. And the next he was once more watching her with that cold, bleak gaze of his. It was disconcerting, the sudden change, like a bank of clouds moving over the sun. She felt as if she should run for cover.

"Well," she said with false brightness. "It's getting late, and I promised to help Millie with dinner tonight."

Nodding curtly, Seth remained where he was. Taylor slid down from the rock, her pencil case in hand. She had taken only a few steps when she realized he still held her sketch pad. She turned around. "Can I have my drawings?"

He held out the pad, but in her hurry to take it and get away, Taylor dropped the book. It dropped to the rock beside Seth, the pages falling open. Too late, Taylor realized the sketches on top were those she had done of Seth.

The sketch was rough—bold lines drawn by an impatient hand. She had caught him a few nights ago as he sat in front of the fire up at the main lodge. His mood had been brooding, intense. And sad, too. At the time Taylor had wondered what could put such a haunted expression on his face. She had chalked it up to his usual gloomy outlook, but her fingers had itched to capture the moment. So she had slipped into a chair across the room, and he hadn't noticed her.

Now he looked down at the drawing, and other expressions skipped across his features. Surprise. Then displeasure. "It's me, but..." He didn't complete the sentence. Instead, he closed the pad and handed it back to Taylor. There was a bitter twist to his lips as he said, "I guess the truth hurts."

She turned without answering him. She was halfway to the lodge before she realized how hard she was clutching the sketch pad to her chest. The truth did hurt. For a few moments she had been fooled into thinking Seth Hardy was human. Warm and human.

But he wasn't.

And that wasn't what she wanted.

She admitted the truth to herself. She was attracted to him. When he had looked at her with eyes so dark, so heavy with sensual intent, a response had quickened deep inside her. No, he wasn't anything like the intellectual, sensitive men she had been attracted to in the past. Seth wasn't so tame, so predictable. In fact, he was as changeable as the weather. But he stirred something in her.

Pausing on the path at the edge of the lodge clearing, Taylor pulled in a deep breath of air. It wasn't *something* that Seth stirred. It was a sexual response. She wanted him. *Wanted* him. The knowledge exploded in her brain. She barely knew this man. She didn't even like him. A sensible, strong-willed woman like herself shouldn't *want* a possessive, primitive man like Seth Hardy.

Cheeks burning, Taylor avoided the lodge and went instead to the cabin she shared with Gerald. She felt off kilter, confused. She needed to think, needed to surround herself with what was most familiar. The familiar parts of her life were thousands of miles away, but this cabin had felt like home from the very beginning. And when she burst through the door, her grandfather was sitting in front of the fire, the most welcome sight she had ever seen.

Then she really looked at him. And she saw the pain that lay over his features like a net. He tried to disguise it, tried to rearrange his expression, but it didn't work.

Temporarily immobilized, she stood just inside the door. "Grandfather?"

He attempted a weak smile. "I'm all right, Taylor. It's just these old bones of mine. I walked too far with Josh."

It was more than that. She knew it was more. "I'm going to get help."

"No." Weak though Gerald looked, that one word rang with authority.

Giving in to his request, she went to him, dropped to her knees beside the chair where he sat. She tried her

best to steady her voice, but the attempt was futile.
"Now I know where Mother and I got our stubborn
independence."

"The curse of the Austins," Gerald murmured.
"We've always been an obstinate bunch." Then he laid
his head back and sighed. His hand reached for hers.
"I feel better just knowing you're here."

So Taylor pulled another chair close to his and sat
beside him, talking quietly until he fell asleep. Even
then she didn't move. She just sat staring at his face.

Because he slept, none of his shields were in place,
and the battle scars life had dealt him showed in every
crease of his skin. Taylor wanted to smooth them
away. What had he been like before illness had taken
its toll? She wished she knew him as Josh did. A vague
resentment started inside her. Up until this point, she
had accepted that her mother, by not contacting Gerald, had done what she thought was best. But Taylor
had been cheated of a relationship with him.

The strength of her feelings for Gerald amazed her.
He had been part of her life for less than two months.
A week ago, she hadn't known what he looked like.
Yet she loved him. She couldn't lose him.

For the second time this afternoon, Taylor could
feel her mother's presence. The sensation was stronger
than it had been at any time since her death. The feeling was so real that Taylor looked up, half expecting
to see Holly. She had never believed in ghosts, but a
floating apparition wouldn't have surprised her at that

moment. She wasn't frightened. She just waited, thinking she might hear something.

The only sounds in the room were the settling of coals in the fireplace and the ticking of the clock on the mantel, but Taylor felt she had to answer an unspoken plea.

"I *won't* lose him," she promised in a fierce whisper.

Determination made her straighten her shoulders, gave her hope.

Seth rarely drank. He had always told Josh that a man who needed alcohol was seeking escape, and only weak men ran away. His attitude had come from years of watching an uncle drink himself into oblivion night after night. Every morning, the man woke up in the same ramshackle house, with too many mouths to feed and too many acres to ranch. The alcohol did nothing, except to make the man meaner than he was before. Seth had sworn never to follow his example.

Tonight, however, he would have gladly escaped into a good bottle of bourbon—not enough to get drunk really, but just enough to dull the senses, to help him sleep.

After only a few fitful hours of rest, he got up, pulled on jeans and wandered into the tiny kitchen of the cabin he shared with Josh. He had given the boy permission to stay in Juneau last night. In all honesty, Seth had wanted his home to himself. But the silence had only served to amplify the many problems confronting him—especially his confusing reactions to Taylor.

He felt old this morning, as old and tired as he had looked in that drawing of Taylor's. Funny, he didn't think of himself that way. Maybe that was just the way he appeared to her. He didn't want that to bother him, but it did.

Grunting, he put a pot of coffee on the stove to perk. He liked his coffee brewed in the old-fashioned way; he didn't like it from an instant powder or dripped through a filter. And he drank it straight, with no sugar or cream to dilute the strong bracing flavor. After his sleepless night, he was going to need several pots to make it through this day.

He had just poured his first cup when the knock sounded at his door. "Damn," he muttered, even as he crossed the room. "Can't they at least wait till five o'clock to hand me a new problem?"

He flung open his door, expecting some fisherman guest needing gear or a tip on where the salmon were running thickest. But it was Taylor who waited on the porch. Taylor, in an oversize black sweater and jeans, her face pale and tear streaked. Taylor, who stared at him with big, panic-stricken eyes.

Terror ripped through him. He stepped outside, grasping her shoulders. "Oh my God, Taylor. Is it Gerald? Taylor, what is it?"

But instead of answering, she stepped into his arms.

Chapter Four

"...Dad says that facing the truth is sometimes the hardest thing a person has to do. I guess I'm facing some truths this summer. I wish he would, too...."

The moment Seth's strong, bare arms closed around her, Taylor realized she was behaving like a fool. But she wanted to be held and comforted. The strength that sustained her yesterday had fled sometime during the sleepless night. In place of hope was only an awful, numbing sorrow. Gerald was going to die. She had only just discovered him, found in him a part of her mother still alive, and now he was going to leave her, too. Finally tiring of tossing in her bed, she had dressed and gone out into the dim, foggy morning. The light in Seth's window had reached out to her. Going into his arms was a reflex.

He held her tight. While the warmth of his body chased the chill from hers, the feel of his bare skin, the musky scent of him brought her back to reality. But even when she realized how foolishly she was behaving, she clung to him. He kept asking her to tell him what was wrong. She resisted, not wanting him to realize there was nothing wrong except her feelings of loss and vulnerability.

"Taylor, please," he murmured, finally pulling away. "Please tell me what's wrong. Is it Gerald?"

She took a deep breath and stepped back, not quite able to look at him. "I'm sorry, Seth. I didn't mean to do that. I didn't mean to frighten you."

"But Gerald—"

"—is fine," she completed. Somehow she found the courage to raise her gaze to his. "As fine as he's ever going to be, that is."

They stood, staring at each other, until Taylor began to shiver.

Seth took her arm. "Come on. You need some coffee."

He sat her down at the round, wooden table in front of the kitchen fire. Only then did Taylor take a good look at him. Her cheeks burned anew.

Shirtless and barefoot, he stood before the stove in jeans that were zipped but not buttoned. They rode low enough on his hips for her to see the line of dark hair that angled down his taut belly. He was unshaven, his hair was mussed and from the puffiness under his eyes, she was willing to bet his night had been just as restless as hers. Loss of sleep looked good on him, however, giving him a rumpled, sex-charged aura.

Pouring coffee into a mug, he said, "I hope you take it black." He turned just in time to catch her blatant stare. He glanced down, as if only then aware of his state of undress. He turned and fastened his jeans before handing her the coffee.

Avoiding his gaze, Taylor took the mug. She concentrated on gulping down as much of the scorching liquid as she could while Seth tossed on a flannel shirt. Hand crooked around his own mug, he settled in the chair opposite hers.

"Now why don't you tell me what's wrong?"

She had to summon some defiance in order to face him. "You know very well what's wrong."

He took a long sip of coffee before answering. "You mean Gerald?"

"Yes. You know he's..." She bit her lip. "He's very ill. When I asked you before, you tap-danced around the truth. You must think I'm stupid, because it's obvious to anyone with eyes that something is terribly, terribly wrong. I just don't know what. He won't tell me. But you know and Millie knows. Josh probably knows. Everyone knows what's going on, but me. But now I want some answers."

Seth looked down at his coffee mug for a long moment before pushing it aside. "Is that what the scene at the door was about?"

Heat once more streaked up her neck to her cheeks. "I said I was sorry about that. I had a terrible night. I saw you and I just, just...lost it for a minute. I'm worried and I'm scared for him." *Damn, but she hadn't meant for her voice to break on that last word.*

Eyes narrowing, Seth sat back in his chair. "Forgive me if I don't buy the theatrics."

She set her mug down so quickly that coffee sloshed over the sides, burning her fingers. The pain was nothing compared to the tears of anger that pricked her eyes. With jerky movements, she got to her feet and turned blindly toward the door. "You're a bastard—did you know that? I don't know why I'm even trying to discuss this with you again."

He caught her before she could take two steps. Hands like steel bands on her arms, he turned her around to face him. "What am I supposed to think about you, anyway? You and your mother ignored the man for years. And now that he's dying, you show up here, full of concern for his welfare. Tell me, Taylor, where were you three years ago when he almost died during bypass surgery?"

"I didn't know anything about him then."

"Your mother did."

She twisted away from him. "Don't you understand? My mother didn't think she could come home. When she left twenty-six years ago, she was pregnant with me. She was in love with a married man. Gerald told her she could never come back. She believed him."

"And what about when he found her?"

The words struck Taylor like a wave, left her struggling for her balance. "He found her?"

"Sure he did." Seth grasped her shoulders again. "Now that you know the man, can you really believe he'd let all these years go by without looking for her?"

She shook her head to clear it. "She never said anything."

Seth's laughter was mirthless. "You mean she never told you the man spent every dime he had looking for her."

"She didn't know. I'm sure she didn't know. He didn't find her."

"Yes, he did," Seth insisted. "He almost lost this place in the process, but he found her about a year after she married your stepfather. He called her and she kept hanging up. He wrote her a letter and she sent it back unopened. Finally, he went to Chicago. She told him to never come near her again. Gerald loved her, but I guess he had too much pride to keep trying in the face of her hatred. He told me years ago that he thought he was doing the best thing for her and for you by just leaving you both alone."

Staring at him in shock, Taylor pressed a hand to her mouth. It wasn't true, couldn't be true. If Gerald had come to her mother with a sincere desire to make amends, Taylor knew Holly wouldn't have sent him away. She knew her mother better than that.

Or did she?

She thought of the diary. That teenaged girl's journal had been a revelation. So much of what Holly had written had little to do with the person Taylor thought her to be. The diary covered nearly four years and a multitude of emotions—passion, bitterness, love, hatred, betrayal. The person who had written that diary had vowed never to forgive her father. Holly had been only seventeen when she'd made that vow, but she hadn't forgiven him. She had told Joe and Taylor that she hated him. And she wouldn't discuss him—ever. Without the diary, it might have been years before Taylor would have found Gerald. If she had even looked. And then it would have been too late.

So maybe Holly had seen Gerald and sent him away.

Turning from Seth, Taylor caught hold of the back of a chair. "What happened when Gerald come to Chicago?"

"You expect me to believe you don't already know?"

Taylor whipped around, wanting with all her heart to slap the derisive smirk from Seth's face. "Why don't you believe me?" she demanded. "I knew almost nothing about him until I found my mother's diary."

"Ah, yes, the elusive diary. Where is it, anyway?"

"In my room, as if that's any of your business."

"You became my business the minute you called Gerald and wanted to come up for a visit. I told you before, I protect what's mine."

"And I told you before, he's as much mine as yours."

Stone-faced, Seth just looked at her.

Frustration crackled through Taylor. "I don't know what I have to do to convince you of why I'm here. I've been telling you from the start that I care about him. Getting to know him is the only reason I made this trip. If you want character witnesses I'll give them to you. But please, please, stop doubting me. If you really care about him, you'll stop."

"But what do you want from him?"

Her breath caught on a sob. "Damn. You just don't get it, do you? I don't want anything."

"Sure you do. Everybody wants something."

For a moment she was silent, studying his taut, controlled features. "Dear God, what happened to make you think something like that? Somebody really took you for a ride, didn't they?" She stepped closer to him. "And I bet it was a woman. Who? Josh's mother? What'd she do?"

"Just stop it." The low-voiced command belied the fury in his face. "We aren't talking about me."

But it didn't stop Taylor. She got right in his face. "Tell me something, Seth. What is it *you* want? If everybody wants something, what's in all this for you?"

He made no reply. But realization hit her with the force of dynamite. Feeling the blood drain from her face, she backed away from him. "I get it now. God, I've been a fool."

"What are you talking about?"

"Maybe you're the one with ulterior motives. Maybe the reason you're upset about me showing up is that now I just might inherit. And then *you'd* have to share the business with me."

She thought he might hit her. His big hands clenched into fists as he came across the room. But he stopped short of touching her again. "How dare you," he muttered. "I would lay down my life for that man."

"How do I know that for sure? I don't know you, remember? The same as you don't know me."

"I've spent fifteen years with him. I don't think that compares to your week. So don't you dare—"

"Dare?" she cut in. "What about the things you dare, Seth. You tried and sentenced me before I ever got off the plane. You haven't given me a chance."

Seth realized then that he was caught in his own trap. She was right. He hadn't give her a chance.

But Taylor wasn't waiting for him to come to his senses. She started for the door. "Maybe we should go to Gerald. You can tell him you think I'm a cold, mercenary bitch, and I'll tell him I think you're eagerly awaiting the reading of his will. What do you think? That should make his last days pretty peaceful, shouldn't it?"

Seth cut her off at the door. "You aren't going to him."

Her eyes blazed up at him. "Despite your tyrannical ways, I don't need your permission to do anything."

"I'd kill you before I let you hurt him like this."

She believed him. He could see that much. He also saw the anger leave her. She closed her eyes and turned away, her shoulders slumping. "Oh, God, I wasn't going to tell him. I wouldn't do that. What does any of this matter, anyway? We're arguing about ourselves. And he's dying." She looked over her shoulder. "He is, isn't he?"

This time Seth left off the fancy footwork. He gave it to her straight. "In April, the doctors said he had a couple of months, at best."

The color left Taylor's cheeks. "I almost missed him," she whispered.

And in that moment Seth knew how wrong all his doubts about her had been. For the pain in her eyes wasn't something he thought anyone—even the greatest actress alive—could fake. A fiery tide of shame swept through him.

He swallowed, trying to find the right words to explain himself.

She didn't give him a chance. Steely determination had already replaced her sorrow. "There has to be something that can be done. What kind of doctors has he seen?"

"The best. I made sure of that."

"But surely somewhere there's someone..."

Once again, Seth took hold of her shoulders, but this time his touch was gentle. "Taylor, everything possible has been done. Gerald's had three bypass surgeries in the past ten years. He did everything they told him to do. But his heart is failing again, and they say they can't risk another operation. Believe me, I made him see the best doctors I could find. He's fought long and hard for his life. And now..." He stopped, his hands slipping from Taylor's shoulders as he tried to control his emotions.

Somehow, her hands ended up in his. Her touch made him look at her. "He shouldn't be here, Seth. He isn't resting. He goes tramping around in the woods with Josh. And at night he doesn't sleep. I hear him up and prowling around at all hours. If something happened, we wouldn't be able to get help in time to save him."

"That's just it. He doesn't want to be saved."

"But that's crazy."

"He made the choice, Taylor. He said he didn't want to spend the last of his life in a hospital bed. He wants to be here, at the lodge. He wants to visit Sarah's grave and walk down to the eagle's nest. He wants to laugh with Josh and Millie and tell his stories to the guests. He said he wanted this one last summer here." Seth drew in a deep breath. "And more than anything, Gerald wanted to see your mother. And you."

Taylor flinched and squeezed her eyes shut, like someone cringing from a blow. "It must have been a shock when Joe called and told him Mom was dead."

Shock was an understatement, but Seth decided not to tell her how close they had come to losing Gerald then. "He took it hard."

"When I called him—"

"He said that call was an answer to a prayer."

Taylor opened her eyes. More green than hazel now, they were filled with tears. "He should have told me how ill he was. I would have come right away."

"You know he wouldn't want you here out of pity."

"Oh, yes," she muttered. "I know that. I know how much pride he has. The same as Mother. Do you know how much their stupid, damn pride cost them?"

Seth knew. For fifteen years, he had watched Gerald struggle with periods of deep despair. He had seen the hollow look come and go in his eyes. He had been at Gerald's side during the first heart attack. He knew Holly's was the name Gerald had called. Several times, Seth had almost contacted her himself. But fearing she would only cause Gerald more pain, he reconsidered. Now he wondered if he had done the right thing. Maybe Holly would have come through for her father.

The gentle pressure of Taylor's fingers gripping his made him look up.

"I'm sorry," she whispered. "I didn't mean what I said about you wanting Gerald's money and the business. I was angry and hurt by your suspicions about me.''

He ducked his head. "I know I can't apologize enough for the way I've treated you. I guess I just got so used to resenting your mother for what she did to Gerald that I expected you to be like her. Even when it was obvious that you aren't...."

"Mother wasn't all bad," Taylor insisted. "What happened between her and Grandfather—it just blew up in their faces. And it kept getting worse." She sighed, then her shoulders straightened. "I guess they both did what they thought was best. Mother may have kept this from me, but otherwise, I've had a great life. I never felt deprived of anything. And you and Gerald and Josh and Millie—you are a family, just as you said. I'm the outsider here."

Shame once again coursed through Seth. "No, Taylor. You're not an outsider."

Because she looked at him with such a lost, grieving expression, it seemed natural to Seth to pull her back into his arms.

In a broken whisper, she said, "I don't want him to die, Seth."

"I know. I know exactly how you feel. I don't want to lose him, either."

"It doesn't seem fair."

"I can't imagine him not being here."

She pressed her face to his shoulder, her voice dropping to no more than a sigh. "Seth."

The way she said his name touched a place in his heart, the place Josh's mother had left bleeding and raw. The place he thought he had sealed forever. Somehow, the slender woman he held had found a spark of life in him. And if he could feel, then he could hurt again. That was reason enough to set Taylor away from him, and he couldn't. She fit against him so well, her head settling on his shoulder, her arms slipping around him. He could feel each shuddering breath she took. Her hair was soft against his cheek. Her scent was as sweet as a spring morning.

He knew his awareness of her as a woman was inappropriate. She was seeking his comfort, not his arousal. Yet he couldn't deny the feelings that tumbled through him. He couldn't stop them. Just as he hadn't wanted to trust her, he didn't want to want her. Yet he did.

Pulling back, she lifted her head. "I wish..." Her words trailed away as they looked at each other.

Her mouth was inches away. Pink. The bottom lip trembling. An invitation written into each curve. Seth considered her mouth for several moments. Too many moments. For she twisted out of his embrace and the chance was lost.

She backed away from him, her laughter shaky and thin. "I'm... I'm sorry, Seth. I've never in my life thrown myself at anyone the way I have with you this morning."

He stepped forward. "Don't worry, it's..." He spread his hands in a helpless gesture as he sought the words to reassure her. "It's really... okay."

"But I don't want you to think that I'm..." She stumbled against a chair, then reached behind her for the door handle. "I'm sorry, Seth. I'm just kind of overwhelmed, you know. I need to think."

"Of course."

"I mean about Gerald. About everything you've told me this morning."

"Sure. I understand. Really, I understand."

She turned, but she didn't quite look at him. "I have to go."

He stepped forward too late to stop her. "Taylor." The door slammed as he said her name. He got to the porch in time to see her dash across the clearing, a slight figure, soon lost in the fog.

Taylor headed for the river, asking herself why she was running away. If he had kissed her, would that have been so awful? The kiss would have been nothing. They were two people, saddened by the impending loss of someone they both loved. The kiss would have been a comfort, nothing more.

Nothing more.

The words mocked her as she paused for breath near her grandmother's grave. Only a fool would believe there was mere comfort in the way Seth had been holding her. And Taylor wasn't a fool. No, she wasn't sophisticated. Her experience with men was limited. But she knew desire. Seth had wanted to kiss her for more reasons than her sorrow over Gerald. For the same reasons she had wanted to kiss him.

She shouldn't be thinking about kissing anyone. All her thoughts should be centered on her grandfather. Now that she was away from Seth, maybe she could think clearly about what should be done.

Folding her arms against her waist, she shivered in the chilly, damp air. The sensible thing would be to go to the cabin or the lodge. But her grandfather would probably be up. Millie would certainly be stirring. Taylor didn't want to face either of them right now. No, she would rather brave the cold and give herself time to collect herself. There was a tree stump around here somewhere. She would sit down and think.

A few minutes later, she gave up on the stump. The closer she got to the river, the thicker the fog became. Around her, the world seemed to be caught in gray swirling clouds. She stuck to what she thought was a path in hopes she would spot a familiar landmark. But nothing registered.

Finally coming to a halt, she glanced over her shoulder, expecting to the see the lights from the lodge. But she must have gone farther than she had thought because she couldn't see a glimmer of light through the heavy fog. It wasn't dark. Days had passed since the Alaska nights had deepened to more than a heavy twilight, but the skies were typically overcast, adding to the gloomy unreality.

To her left, there was a crash in the undergrowth. Thinking of bears, Taylor shrank back against a tree.

But as the figure materialized in the gray mist, she saw it was distinctly human.

"Taylor?" Gerald said, coming toward her. "Is that you?"

"Grandfather, what are you doing out in this damp air?"

He chuckled. "It's pretty hard to live in southeast Alaska and avoid damp air."

"But you should be in bed."

"And miss the morning? No, thank you." Coming close enough for her to see his face clearly, he peered at her in a quizzical way. "I might ask what you're doing out, though. I could have been a bear."

"Which is why you shouldn't be out here, either."

"Oh, the bears in this forest know me. They know I gave up hunting for sport years ago. Why, I'm almost sure I've encountered that brown bear Josh saw the other day. He said it walked kind of funny, like one of its front legs is shorter than the other. I believe I met up with it five or six years ago. I was on a walk up into the mountains..."

While he rambled into one of his many stories, Taylor took a deep breath. This was exactly the reason why he belonged in a hospital. When he felt well, he overdid it. Then he paid for it later with an episode like the one she had witnessed yesterday afternoon at the cabin. And if he took off into the forest, they might never find him.

"Grandfather," she said, cutting into his story. "I wish you wouldn't do this."

He looked at her in surprise. "Do what, Taylor?"

"Wander off all the time. You could get hurt or lost."

He chuckled. "Lost? I couldn't get lost around here. This is my home. I know it just the way you know downtown Chicago."

"But—"

"Taylor," he interrupted in a gentle tone. "It's nice to have you worry about me, but I know what I'm doing."

She couldn't doubt him. Not when she looked into his luminous eyes. As always, those eyes calmed her, reassured her.

He held out his hand. "Come on, I was going to visit the eagle."

Taylor tucked her arm through his as they set off down the path. "How do you know where he is?"

"Why the nest is just down here." The direction he pointed in was the opposite of the one Taylor would have chosen.

"But a minute ago I couldn't even see the lodge."

Gerald clucked in disapproval. "Goodness, girl, the lodge is right up there." He pointed to his right, and sure enough, lights gleamed through a mist that was beginning to clear.

That seemed proof indeed that Gerald knew the right direction to take. A few more bends in the path brought them to the eagle's nest, clearly visible in the rapidly disintegrating fog. Side by side, Taylor and Gerald sat on the broad rock, listening to the early morning sounds. Perhaps fifteen minutes passed before the bird's distinctive cry came from overhead.

"So the lazybones is finally getting up," Gerald murmured.

Again the eagle's cry rang through the still morning air. In a flurry of wings, it flew from the nest and circled above. Then it was gone, disappearing into the remaining fog like a vision.

Taylor didn't realize she was holding her breath until she released it in a long sigh. "I think he knows who you are, Grandfather."

"Of course he does."

"Does anyone ever tame an eagle?"

"And why would anyone want to tame something so wild and beautiful? Eagles belong in the forests, beside rivers, not as someone's pet, not even perched on a pole in a zoo. There are those who would disagree with me, but I believe that's crueler than death."

The same sentiments could be applied to him, she realized. That was the reason he wasn't in a hospital somewhere. Her grandfather belonged to the forest and the river, to this land he and his Sarah had carved from the wilderness. Just as he had found his way unerringly through the fog, he knew how he wanted to spend the last few days of his life.

Earlier, when Seth was busy explaining all this to her, she hadn't really believed him. She had thought she could convince Gerald to go somewhere to seek additional medical attention. Now she knew she was wrong.

The fighter in her, the person her mother had raised, wanted to struggle against the inevitable. But Taylor was wise enough to know this really wasn't her fight. The choice of his life or death belonged to Gerald.

She slipped her hand into his. "I'm glad I found you."

"So am I." Slowly, almost reverently, he smoothed the hair back from her forehead and smiled.

"Mother used to do that," Taylor said. "When I was sick or upset or I just wanted to be with her, she would stroke my hair just like that. It always helped."

"She was a good mother?"

"The absolute best."

"Then maybe I didn't fail her completely."

"No, you didn't."

A cry sounded overhead, and together they looked up as the eagle returned to its nest, breakfast clutched in its talons.

There were a hundred things Taylor wanted to say; she especially wanted to ask questions about what had happened when Gerald found Holly in Chicago. But now didn't seem the right time. And what was past couldn't be any more important than the few, precious days left to be with Gerald.

She couldn't talk about his death. All she could manage was, "The eagle's going to miss you, Grandfather." Her own feelings went without saying.

Gerald made no reply, but his hand tightened on hers.

* * *

At the edge of the path, Seth faded back among the trees. The two people sitting so close together on the rock hadn't noticed him.

After Taylor left him, he had dressed and gone after her. When she wasn't at Gerald's cabin or the lodge, he started down one path and then another, worrying about her getting lost in the fog.

In truth, he didn't know why he had followed her at all. The last thing he needed was to become more entangled with her. She had used her head this morning, stopping before they indulged in a foolish kiss. Neither of them had anything to regret.

But he regretted.

He wished they had been foolish.

And he yearned to indulge the impulse that had brought Taylor's mouth so close to his own.

Seth hadn't wasted many moments of his life on dreams. But he stood alone in the forest long after Taylor and Gerald were gone, and all of his thoughts were wasted on her.

Chapter Five

"...I found out more about him in a day than in the years I've known everyone else. I never thought it could happen so fast...."

Seth wasn't eager to face Taylor again. He did everything he could—including inventing problems—to stay busy and out of her way.

It didn't work.

He had always liked what he did—supervising the maintenance of the planes, boats and buildings, scheduling pilots, conferring with Millie on food costs and housekeeping problems. Occasionally, he was called on to lead fishing expeditions or take the controls for a tourist group's flight over the glacier ice fields. Since Gerald's health had deteriorated, he had taken over the bookkeeping, as well. In summers past, at least three different catastrophes cropped up every day that demanded his attention.

But this year the place ran like a well-oiled machine. Josh still gave him a hard time about wanting to be in Juneau as much as possible, but the boy also kept up with his chores, virtually taking over any maintenance problems. Allison and an older woman handled the Juneau office. The two female and two male college students who helped with fishing trips, hikes, kitchen duty and housekeeping were veterans from previous summers' employment. Millie, of course, was organized to the point of irritation. And a computer system had cut his bookkeeping and other paperwork in half. That left Seth with more time than he'd had in years.

Time to listen for Taylor's laugh.

Time to study her face in the firelit shadows of the lodge's main hall.

Time to relive those moments when he had held her close.

More than a week had passed since that foggy, intense morning. Taylor was everywhere Seth turned. Truly avoiding her would have meant avoiding Gerald, as well, and that was something Seth didn't want.

Over the years, he and the older man had spent many an hour in front of the fire, drinking coffee and talking about subjects that ranged from the economy to the possibility of sunshine the next day, from the advisability of buying a new outboard motor to *glasnost*. Taylor slipped easily into their routine. Josh joined them sometimes. Millie, too. But as often as not, it was just Gerald and Taylor and Seth, talking, sometimes until late in the evening.

Seth already knew Taylor was intelligent and thoughtful. What surprised him was how much they had in common—decidedly moderate political views, an affection for folk-rock music and an addiction to horror novels. Even then there were points of contention. One evening they argued until 2:00 a.m. about the true meaning of a favorite Stephen King novel. Only the mantel clock striking the hour ended the debate.

Taylor had stretched and yawned, turning to Gerald. "Well, I guess Seth and I have been on a tangent long enough."

But Gerald didn't answer. His chair was empty. Sometime during the argument he had wandered off to bed, unnoticed by Seth or Taylor.

"I guess I'm more boring than I thought," Seth said, laughing.

Laying her head against the back of the leather couch where she was snuggled, Taylor had smiled. "I wasn't bored."

They sat, just looking at each other, grinning. Seth was reminded, oddly enough, of the day in the sixth grade when he had discovered he really liked to talk to girls. The moment had that kind of wonder, that kind of surprise.

Yet the warm intimacy of that night bedeviled him, too. He kept thinking of Taylor, curled like a contented cat into the corner of the couch, with sleepy eyes and a sweet smile. He wondered what she would have done if he had crossed the room and kissed her.

He developed a peculiar awareness of her. He found he could sit in the lodge's office and pick out her light, quick footsteps as she crossed the broad-planked floor. He could tell from her tone of voice whether she was talking to Gerald or to Josh. One day Seth stood for a good ten minutes or more by the kitchen window, pretending to check a supply list, but in reality watching Taylor and fascinated by the way she chewed on her bottom lip as she followed Millie's instructions on making biscuits.

He caught her watching him often. At dinner, when he sat swapping war stories with one of the pilots who was also a Vietnam vet. Or afterward, when the guests gathered in the hall to socialize or to listen to Gerald talk about his encounters with bears, wolves and moose. Seth had never in his life believed anything he had heard about gazes meeting across crowded rooms. He did now.

Even in the cabin with Josh, there was no escape. His son was Taylor's biggest fan, making plans for activities she might enjoy, quoting her at every turn. Her drawing of the eagle held a place of honor in the boy's bedroom.

Seth told himself he was fascinated by Taylor because he had gone too long without a woman. Over the years, there had been several women in Juneau who were willing to share their beds with him. He always ended the relationship before the woman started to count on him. He supposed that attitude had earned him something of a reputation. Since Josh had gotten older and started attending high school in Juneau, Seth had become more discreet. It was just as well. His interest in casual liaisons had waned over the past year.

But one night, when thoughts of Taylor drove him to near distraction, he went into Juneau. He made it all the way to a small café owned by a woman with whom he had kept company many times in the past.

Bobbie Jo had bright red hair and sparkling green eyes. She was a pretty woman, close to Seth's age, a grown-up flower child who had wandered to Alaska years ago in search of clean air and clear water. She was independent to the point of militancy. Undemanding yet interesting, she had amused Seth once upon a time. They had shared some laughs and some great sex.

Clearly happy to see him on this rainy night, she showed him to a booth near the back of her small, colorful restaurant. "It's been months since you've darkened the door. Busy?"

"'Tis the season. I'm sure it's the same for you, too."

"More people come through every year. I guess it's harder than ever to find a vacation spot that's not clogged with concrete and plastic."

He chuckled. "That'll never happen around here. Not if you can help it, right?" Bobbie Jo was an ardent environmentalist, a person who backed her ideals with real action. She recycled. She harassed legislators for tougher laws. She had closed her restaurant in order to help with the oil-spill cleanup.

The light flashed on her gold loop earrings as she laughed. "That reminds me. I have a petition about the Brazilian rain forests that I'd like you to sign."

He laughed and ordered dinner, lingering over coffee. Bobbie Jo flirted with him, just as she always did. In years past, the evening would have culminated in the tiny apartment over the restaurant. But at the end of this evening, Seth left Bobbie Jo's warmth and color behind him and went back out into the rain.

At the corner he paused to look back at the restaurant. Bobbie Jo stood in the doorway, her hair a flaming red in the light that streamed into the gloomy evening. She waved. He knew he could turn around and stay at her place until breakfast. It might be pleasant. But he knew it wouldn't be enough. So he saluted the woman in the doorway and drew his slicker tight against the rain. He hurried to his plane and flew home.

Home. Where Taylor invaded every corner.

He needed an escape. Instead, Gerald handed him an additional sentence.

The bomb dropped one morning after breakfast in the lodge dining room. Most of the guests had scattered, and Seth and Millie were enjoying a cup of coffee when Taylor and Gerald appeared. Taylor went into the kitchen, while Gerald crossed to Seth and Millie's table.

Seth realized the older man looked better than he had in months. His eyes were clear, his color improved. Obviously he was glorying in the time spent with his granddaughter.

"Well this is a pleasure," Millie said, as Gerald took the chair opposite hers. "You and Taylor have been breakfasting alone these past few days."

Gerald chuckled. "Yes, and I think she's getting pretty tired of toast, instant coffee and my company."

Millie beamed. "I doubt that your company is wearing on the girl."

"I want her to get out and see more of the area." Gerald looked at Seth. "You're still going to take her about, aren't you?"

Seth had managed to forget Gerald's request that he show Taylor around. "I'm sure Josh would love to do it, Gerald. There's a lot going on here, and I—"

"What do you mean?" Millie demanded.

"Just that I'm busy, and I think—"

Blue eyes snapping, Millie cut him off again. "If you're so busy, why are we sitting here drinking coffee in the middle of the morning?"

"It's barely eight."

"I remember a time when we had both done a half a day's work by this hour, so don't be going on about how busy you are." Millie patted Gerald's hand. "Don't you worry. I'll make sure Seth shows your girl a good time."

"But Josh would—"

"Goodness, Seth," Millie exclaimed. "Anyone would think you were trying to avoid Taylor. And why ever would you do that?"

There was a peculiar gleam in the woman's eye that told Seth she might know exactly why he would want to avoid Taylor. He should have known Millie would miss nothing that went on around here. Irritated, he started to mount another protest.

Gerald frowned. "Seth, I didn't think I was asking too big a favor."

Millie's derisive snort underscored his remark. "Since when is spending time with a pretty woman a favor?"

Seth tried one more avenue of escape. "Has anyone asked Taylor if she even wants to go sightseeing? I mean, she came to be with you, Gerald."

"But I want her to see the land," Gerald insisted. "And even though I'm . . . I'm feeling well these days, I can't take her to the places I want her to go. I want you to do it."

Seth wasn't sure he understood. He thought his friend was asking him to do more than conduct a sightseeing tour.

The man's next words confirmed that suspicion. He looked Seth straight in the eye. "You're the only one I trust to show her everything the way it should be shown."

As Seth had pointed out to Millie time and again, Gerald had always known exactly how to wrap all of them around his finger. Seth couldn't deny him much, especially now. "All right," he agreed gruffly. "I'll take Taylor—"

"Take me where?"

He looked up and into Taylor's eyes. Having slipped in from the kitchen without any of them noticing, she stood sipping a cup of coffee. She looked younger than ever this morning, her face freshly scrubbed, her hair free about her face, the ends still damp from her shower. Her gaze skipped from his to the others at the table. "What's going on?"

"There are a couple of places I want Seth to take you," Gerald explained.

She darted another quick look at him as she set her coffee mug and a bowl of cereal on the table. "What places, Grandfather?"

"Seth knows."

A thin line forming between her brows, she took the seat opposite Seth's. "That sounds awfully mysterious."

"You'll see," was all Gerald would say.

Seth knew when he was beaten. He stood. "Taylor, what's your shoe size?"

"What?"

"You're going to need some rubber hiking boots for where we're going today."

"I have boots."

"Do they go to your knees? We're going to get into some mud, probably. You'll need some dancing shoes."

"Dancing shoes?"

Millie explained, "We Southeasterners call knee-high rubber boots 'dancing shoes.' They sure do help you dance up the muddy trails."

Wondering exactly what she was letting herself in for, Taylor gave Seth her shoe size.

He turned to go. "We've got something around here that will fit you. Meet me behind the lodge in about an hour. And bring a jacket. The sun's out now, but I imagine it will rain."

With a perplexed frown, Taylor watched him leave. He didn't look any too thrilled with the idea of showing her these unknown places Gerald wanted her to see. In truth, she wasn't sure how she felt about spending more time in his company. In the past week, she had tried her best to forget their almost-kiss. It wasn't easy considering he seemed to be less than an arm's length away at any given moment. It was especially difficult since she had discovered he could be such good company.

For Gerald's sake, it would be nice if she and Seth became friends. But what existed between them didn't feel like friendship. Something happened to the atmosphere each time they were together. The very air grew heavy. Like on a summer's day in Chicago before a thunderstorm.

Still frowning, she looked up at Gerald and Millie. Both sported enigmatic smiles. "What is it?"

The two exchanged even more puzzling glances, then Millie got up. "I think I'll go pack you and Seth a picnic lunch."

"Surely we'll be back before lunch."

The woman giggled. "I wouldn't count on it."

Taylor looked at her grandfather. "What are the two of you up to?"

"Nothing, of course."

She didn't believe him. But a couple of hours later, she forgot to worry about what Gerald and Millie might be plotting. She followed Seth up a steep path high above the valley where the lodge and its collection of buildings lay. The valley was to their right, bordered by the river and still more mountains. Seth pointed far in the distance, where a glacier gleamed white and blue. Her grandfather had told her the glacier was growing, advancing day by day, inch by inch.

From the lodge, the glacier looked too far away to ever threaten the lodge. But from up here, the moving mountains of ice appeared ready to crush the tiny slice of civilization.

"What happens when it fills up the valley?" she asked Seth, when they paused for moment.

He looked up from adjusting the straps on his backpack to the direction she pointed. "That could take a hundred years at the rate the scientists say it's moving. Or it could stop growing, start retreating, carving out an even bigger valley."

"So if I came back here, years from now, the view might be different."

She felt, rather than saw, the long look Seth gave her before he answered. "There are changes all the time. They're gradual, though."

"Has it changed since you first came here?"

Eyes narrowed, he turned, his gaze sweeping the panorama spread before them. "Not really. Except now I know it's my home."

There was something warm in his expression, a tone in his deep voice than appealed to Taylor. He had started out this morning as the same taciturn individual she had met weeks ago. She supposed he was more determined than she to forget the moments she had spent in his arms. But the higher they had climbed, the more of his reserve he shed. She thought he might even be enjoying himself.

Absurdly pleased by that knowledge, Taylor took a deep breath. The air was cooler here than in the valley. The breeze felt as if it blew straight off the snow that capped the mountains, to their backs. She didn't know that she had ever breathed air this clear or pure. City smog was going to be a shock to her system when she went back. In Chicago, late-June heat would be pressing in on the residents. Her weekly letter from Joe had said they were having record-setting temperatures. Taylor was glad to be escaping the heat and humidity. She missed her stepfather, his new wife and the rest of her adoptive family and close friends. But the city? No, the city didn't hold the appeal it had only a few weeks ago.

She gazed out across the valley again. How quickly this land could wrap itself around a person's heart.

"Come on," Seth urged. "We've still got a lot of ground to cover before we get where we're going."

"And where is that?"

He looked over his shoulder at her, his expression as mysterious as Gerald's had been. "You'll know we're there when you see it."

She grunted in reply, saving her breath for their continued climb above the valley. Besides their steady, labored breaths, the only sound was the jingle of the bells Seth had tied to their packs as a warning to any bears who might be in the vicinity. Their route had taken them over the small, densely wooded ridges immediately behind the lodge and up the side of a mountain. Now they began another descent into the lush rain forest.

Spruce, hemlock and cedar trees blanketed the land, their scents mingling with the pungent odors of damp, rich earth and the proliferation of plants. The colors were as verdant as in any Rousseau masterpiece. Taylor yearned to stop and attempt some sketches, but Seth pressed on down the overgrown trail.

Most everything was green, in shades that ranged from lime to the deepest emerald. And there were hints of other colors, too. One particularly beautiful plant glowed golden in the underbrush. Exclaiming over its beauty, Taylor bent to explore its texture. Seth stopped her, however, and carefully pointed out the nasty, stinging thorns she hadn't noticed.

"Devil's club," he called it. "I've seen some deep cuts on people whose curiosity got the best of them."

Thereafter, Taylor was content to look and not touch.

The path turned upward again. It was steep and muddy. Much as she wanted to operate under her own steam, she had to allow Seth to pull her along behind him in places. He told her the path would turn into a stream if it rained hard enough.

Though the sky was fairly blue now, Taylor had been in the southeast long enough to know how quickly that could change. "What will we do if it does rain hard?"

He only laughed at her dismay. "I guess we'll be trapped up here."

That dismaying prospect occupied her thoughts for the rest of the steep ascent. Then she saw their destination. And wonder quickly replaced every other thought.

The lake was small, its color graduating from deep green to blue-gray, a reflection of the surrounding forest and the sky above. Taylor's first thought was that they had stumbled across a little patch of heaven that had fallen from above.

"Maybe this wouldn't be such a bad place to be trapped," she murmured.

Seth agreed, but when she turned, she saw that he was looking at her rather than the scene spread before them.

His steady regard unnerved her, but she wasn't the one who looked away first. "Come on," he said gruffly, "let's see what Millie packed for lunch."

They set their backpacks down in a clearing that bordered the water. Yellow-gold water lilies decorated one corner of the lake. The blossoms shimmered in the weak sunlight, but remained well beyond Taylor's reach as she bent to wash her hands in the water. She splashed some on her face, too. It felt as clean and cold as snow. The sensation made her laugh, and from the trees a group of ravens rose with loud complaints and the flurry of wings.

"You've irritated the residents," Seth told her. "We'd better watch out. They'll probably tell the local bears that we've invaded the territory."

Taylor had seen a couple of brown bears in the past weeks. They lumbered into the lodge area most every day, attracted by the scent of the salmon Millie and her helpers grilled outdoors. Everyone gave the big, brown animals a wide berth, but no one seemed particularly afraid of them, either. "I think all of you are just trying to scare me about the bears."

"Just take my advice and try to stay away from them."

She saluted him smartly and dropped to her knees beside the backpack she had shed. "At the moment

I'm hungry enough to fight a bear over his berries. We've been walking for almost four hours.''

For lunch, Millie had packed cold fried chicken, the dill pickles she canned herself, plus celery and carrot sticks and her special homemade bread, spread thick with honey butter. Taylor ate almost as much as Seth, until, groaning, she lay back, bundling her backpack into a pillow for her head. The sun was just warm enough, and her jacket provided protection from the damp, mossy ground. Through half-opened eyes, she watched Seth place all their scraps in plastic bags and tuck them away in his own pack.

"We really don't want to attract any bears," he offered by way of explanation.

Taylor murmured a response. The scene before her was too beautiful for her to even consider the possibility of a bear disturbing them. "I think I understand why Grandfather wanted me to see this."

Reclining against his own pack, Seth nodded. "He told me it was Sarah's favorite spot."

"It's easy to understand why."

Seth sighed. "A lot of things have happened up here."

She looked at him with interest. "Like what."

"Well, Gerald said your mother ran away and spent two nights up here once."

"Two nights? Wasn't he frantic?"

"Oh, he found her. He staked out a place in the woods and kept an eye on her till she ran out of food. He said he thought she would have stayed longer if she hadn't forgotten her fishing rod. The lake's full of trout."

"I can't imagine Mom alone up here for two days."

Seth shrugged. "She grew up here, she knew the dangers and how to take care of herself. Josh heard Gerald tell the story enough times that he decided to try it himself, once."

"Did you hide in the woods and watch out for him?"

"Nope, I joined him. We stayed up here for a couple of days, living on fish and trail mix. We had a great time." He sat up, rubbing a hand across his jaw as he looked out at the lake. Almost to himself, he said, "Maybe we'll do that again. At the end of the season, maybe...."

Taylor could understand the desire to escape to this place. It was magic. She could feel it in the air. She wanted to capture it, take the feeling away with her. "I have to sketch this place," she decided aloud.

"What about the eagle's nest?"

"That comes first, of course. I promised Grandfather. But there are so many other places I want to set down on paper. I guess a person could spend a lifetime trying to put Alaska on canvas."

"And you've only seen one little corner of the state. You've flown over the glaciers, but you haven't sailed right up to the face of one."

"I can do that?"

"Sure. You can take a helicopter up and walk on them, too."

"I don't know," she said, thinking of the vast, rough-looking ice fields. "Is it safe?"

"Sure. Half the tourists who visit do it." He warmed to his subject. "To me, it feels the way I always imagined walking on the moon would be. The crevasses you see from the air are like deep, narrow craters. A person could topple into one of them and never be seen again." He grinned at her shiver of fright. "You can't leave Alaska without a glacier walk."

She turned on her side, propping her head on her hand. "What else should I do?"

"Fish for salmon, of course. Go killer whale watching up in Glacier Bay. And maybe go up to Mt. McKinley. If you're lucky and the weather is good, you'll see the peak. From there, you can go into Fairbanks. Today is the summer solstice. They'll have twenty-two hours of daylight."

"Aren't we having the same here?"

"Not like there, or up at the top of the continent at Barrow. You've heard of the midnight sun? It's true— the sun just almost touches the horizon. Then it bounces back up. It's incredible." Seth grinned then, sheepishly. "Sorry—I don't usually go on like a tour guide."

Taylor smiled. "I asked, remember? You sound as if you've traveled the state."

He shook his head. "I haven't seen a tenth of it."

"But you're going to, right?"

"Maybe." His gaze again lifted to the lake. "I'm pretty happy being here. Before I came to work for Gerald, I spent about a year rambling around the state. I didn't think I was looking for a home, but..." He included the lake and the surrounding mountains in his sweeping gesture. "This is where home turned out to be."

"Especially when Josh came to live with you?"

He didn't question how she had come to know Josh hadn't always been with him. And the softening of his features gave her his answer.

She paused, wondering if Seth's expansive mood would entertain any personal questions. She decided to risk it, deliberately keeping her tone casual. "What brought you here, anyway?"

He stretched his long legs out in front of him. "The same thing that brings most people—adventure. I was in the air force in Vietnam. I spent most of my time on the crew of a cargo plane. I found that pretty boring. When I came out of the service, I just wanted to fly. I was a flight instructor for a while in California, but that wasn't much of a challenge. A buddy told me there were lots of opportunities for pilots here in Alaska. So I sold everything I had, came up here, bought my first plane and eventually went to work with Gerald."

"I gather you were a pilot before you went into the air force."

"I had been flying smaller craft since I was twelve." She sat up. "Twelve? Isn't that a little young?"

"I taught Josh when he was ten."

"Your parents must have developed some premature gray hair over you."

"They didn't care." His statement was bitter, his expression darkening.

Taylor didn't press for details. Expansive or not, Seth wasn't a man you could push. She was silent for moment, looking at the lake instead of at him. Very casually she asked, "What got you into flying?"

He surprised her with his ready answer. "There was an airstrip near the town where I went to school. Montana's a lot like Alaska, in a way—a lot of wide-open spaces. Some ranchers use helicopters or planes to cover the distances."

"Your family had a plane?"

His laugh was short. "Hardly. We were a small spread in relation to some of the big boys. Dad and my brothers could cover the place pretty well by horse or truck."

"So you were a cowboy growing up." The image fit him.

Again his mouth tightened. "I wasn't a cowboy. I just grew up. On my own, mostly. My mother died when I was about a year old. My brothers were a lot older—ten years and more. Dad was too busy to deal with an unexpected child." He shrugged, but she didn't think the careless gesture reflected his true feelings.

Sympathetic words sprang to her lips, but something in his face made her swallow them. She didn't expect him to continue, but he did, explaining in dull, almost emotionless tones that he had spent most of his time with an aunt and uncle who owned the ranch near his father's.

"Aunt Shirley already had six kids. I guess one more was no big deal. She was nice enough, but she had a lot to contend with." He rubbed his hands down his denim-clad thighs and laughed, a sound that held no mirth. Then his hands clenched into fists. "I just tried to stay out of the way, mostly. Uncle Luther had a nasty temper when he drank. And he drank all the time."

A tight ball of pain formed in Taylor's chest as the picture of his childhood materialized. She could see in his face the loneliness he must have endured. Every child deserved to be something more than "no big deal." How could his father have abandoned Seth to such a fate?

However, there was a faraway, dreamy look in his eyes as he told her about the man who owned the local airstrip. "Everything changed the first time Mr. Whittaker took me up with him. I knew right then that I was going to fly right out of that town."

His determined voice echoed around the lake, jerking Seth back to reality. He rarely talked about his background. It was over and done with. He could never imagine why anyone would be interested. "Sorry," he mumbled. "I didn't mean to ramble on."

"You weren't rambling," Taylor said, leaning forward, her pretty features alight with curiosity. "What happened next?"

Seth shook his head. "Nothing interesting."

"Wait a minute. You went from a small town in Montana to—and I'm quoting what you told me a few weeks ago—'Honolulu, Tokyo and Saigon.' That sounds pretty interesting to me."

"Yeah, well, the air force and Vietnam provide some wonderful travel opportunities."

"In which one of those cities was Josh born?"

This question cut just a little too close to some of his deepest scars. So instead of answering, he strode off toward the lake, leaving Taylor alone.

What was it about the woman that had induced him to spill his guts that way? Perhaps it was a talent she had inherited from Gerald, who on long winter nights, had often prodded Seth into talking far too much about himself. But it was different with Gerald. With him, Seth had nothing to lose. With Taylor...well, he felt if he opened himself too wide, she would find a way to get inside his carefully constructed life.

As if she wasn't already inside.

Seizing a rock from the edge of the lake, Seth sent it skipping across the gray, glassy surface. Ripples spread outward, disturbing the water's perfect reflection of the surrounding mountains. Taylor was like that stone. She had dropped into his life only weeks ago, but ever since, he had been rocking from the impact of her presence. She was an unneeded complication in a life already disturbed enough by his son's growing pains and Gerald's illness. He was drawn to her in ways he had hoped to never be drawn to a woman again. Nothing would come of the attraction. He couldn't let anything develop.

With a defeated sigh, Seth glanced at his watch. It was time to go. Slowly he walked back to where Taylor still sat.

While he had been lost in contemplation, she had opened her sketch pad and was now absorbed in her work. In response to his suggestion that they leave, she asked, "Can you give me a few minutes?"

He gave his assent with a grunt; he was impatient to be off, yet also fascinated by watching her work. Brow furrowed, bottom lip caught between her teeth, she sent her pencil flying across the page, the lines giving definition to the mountains and the lake they cradled. Sitting beside her, surrounded by the small sounds and deep silences of the land, Seth knew an incredible sense of well-being. He would have liked to stay here forever.

But they couldn't. Gerald might worry, or worse, might need them. Being out of contact with the lodge with Gerald's condition as it was probably wasn't a good idea. And they needed to try and beat the rain, too. The sun had disappeared behind gray clouds, so a downpour was probably in the offing.

"We have to go," Seth told Taylor. When she again asked for one minute more, he added, "You don't want to get caught in a downpour on that first path down. It might turn into a waterfall.''

She groaned, closed her sketch pad and stood, shrugging into her jacket.

Seth had his jacket on and was reaching for his backpack when he saw the two brown bear cubs. They were off to the right, perhaps half the circumference of the lake away, and like teddy bears brought to life, they were gamboling through the meadow's grass.

Nodding in the cub's direction, Seth took hold of Taylor's arm. "Come on, get your pack and let's get out of here."

"They're adorable," she breathed.

"Yeah, but where baby is, Mother can't be far..." His words died as he looked to the left. On the other side of the lake, not far from the path they needed to take, was an adult bear. She was feeding on berries and didn't seem to have heard or noticed the human intruders. She was some distance away, but Seth and Taylor were in between a mother and her young. And there was no more dangerous place to be when it came to bears.

Seth cursed softly. He should have been on the lookout instead of absorbed in watching Taylor.

"Turn around," he said. "Slowly."

To her credit, Taylor did as he asked. Her eyes widened at the sight of the mother bear. "What do we do?"

Making no quick moves, Seth crouched down. He kept his eyes on the mother while he took hold of the bells on his backpack. With her cubs so close by, he didn't want to startle the mother with any noise. She might decide he and Taylor were a threat. Smothering the bells' sound in the palm of his hand, he jerked them loose and shoved them into his pocket. Then he picked up the backpack, and with one hand on Taylor's arm, began to back into the forest.

"What about my pack?" Taylor murmured.

"Leave it. I've got everything we need."

Just as they reached the edge of the forest, the bear stopped her berry feast and drew herself up. Front claws waved as her massive nose lifted into the air.

"Damn, I think she smells us," Seth muttered.

The animal's growl, loud as thunder to Taylor's ears, rent the air. She wanted to run. But Seth continued to move them slowly, carefully, into the dense woods. The bear dropped to all fours. A cold sweat broke out on Taylor's forehead.

Seth's voice was soft against her ear. "Steady, now. Just keep moving. She's not sure where or what we are."

The bear moved forward, then broke into a gallop, heading toward the woods. Near Taylor's discarded backpack, the bear stopped, rearing up on her hind legs.

But Seth kept moving them backward. Slowly, steadily. Away from the claws that again pawed the air. Taylor's heart thudded against her ribs. At any moment the bear was going to lurch forward, into the woods. At any moment, those claws would rake down Seth's chest. She started to pray.

But the bear backed down. She nosed the backpack. With a last warning growl, she dropped to all fours again and took off around the lake toward her cubs.

Seth's hand fastened on Taylor's forearm in a painful grip. "Walk," he ordered tersely. "Don't run. But haul ass, all the same."

Somehow, Taylor kept pace with his long strides. They had to fight their way through thick undergrowth, but Seth eventually found their trail. He stopped once, to store her sketch pad in the pack and reattach the warning bells. They rang through the still air, but neither Taylor nor Seth spoke.

The rain started near the middle of the steepest part of the trail. The path didn't become a waterfall, as Seth had warned. But they slipped and slid their way to the bottom. It wasn't until then that Taylor allowed herself to believe they weren't being followed by the bear. The relief buckled her legs. Seth caught her before she could fall.

Water cascaded over them. Even after he pulled her to the shelter of a particularly dense stand of trees, cold wind-driven rain pelted them from all sides. They stood in the deluge, holding onto each other like the last two survivors of an epic disaster.

When Seth lowered his mouth to hers, he tasted like the rain.

NO RISK, NO OBLIGATION TO BUY...NOW OR EVER!

GUARANTEED

PLAY "ROLL A DOUBLE" AND GET AS MANY AS FIVE GIFTS!

HERE'S HOW TO PLAY:

1. Peel off label from front cover. Place it in space provided at right. With a coin, carefully scratch off the silver dice. This makes you eligible to receive two or more free books, and possibly another gift, depending on what is revealed beneath the scratch-off area.

2. You'll receive brand-new Silhouette Special Edition® novels. When you return this card, we'll rush you the books and gift you qualify for ABSOLUTELY FREE!

3. Then, if we don't hear from you, every month, we'll send you 6 additional novels to read and enjoy. You can return them and owe nothing, but if you decide to keep them, you'll pay only $2.96 per book—a saving of 43¢ each off the cover price.

4. When you subscribe to the Silhouette Reader Service™, you'll also get our newsletter, as well as additional free gifts from time to time.

5. You must be completely satisfied. You may cancel at any time simply by sending us a note or a shipping statement marked "cancel" or by returning any shipment to us at our expense.

The Austrian crystal sparkles like a
diamond! And it's carefully set in a romantic
"Key to Your Heart" pendant on a generous
18" chain. The entire necklace is yours free
as added thanks for giving our Reader
Service a try!

"ROLL A DOUBLE!"

PLACE LABEL HERE

SCRATCH HERE

**SEE CLAIM CHART
BELOW**

235 CIS AELS
(U-SIL-SE-05/92)

YES! I have placed my label from the front cover into the space
provided above and scratched off the silver dice. Please rush me
the free books and gift that I am entitled to. I understand that I am
under no obligation to purchase any books, as explained on the
opposite page.

NAME _____

ADDRESS _____ APT. _____

CITY _____ STATE _____ ZIP CODE _____

DETACH AND MAIL CARD TODAY!

SILHOUETTE "NO RISK" GUARANTEE

- You're not required to buy a single book—ever!
- You must be completely satisfied or you may cancel at any time simply by sending us a note or shipping statement marked "cancel" or by returning any shipment to us at our cost. Either way, you will receive no more books; you'll have no obligation to buy.
- The free books and gift you claimed on this "Roll A Double" offer remain yours to keep no matter what you decide.

If offer card is missing, please write to: Silhouette Reader Service, 3010 Walden Ave., P.O. Box 1867, Buffalo, NY 14269-1867

Fear receded as the kiss deepened. Heat replaced the cold. With his kiss, Seth found depths Taylor hadn't known existed inside her. The two of them blended together and with the elements until she wasn't sure where she or he or the wind or the rain ended or began. They could have kissed for hours. Or minutes. Or only a second. She didn't know that any means of measuring time could be applied. There was only the kiss and then Seth's voice, saying her name again and again in the tradition-honored litany of a man and woman caught by passion.

When at last they drew apart, the wind still blew rain into their faces. Seth started to speak, to say the sane, reasonable words Taylor was certain she didn't want to hear. So she kissed him again.

He drew away eventually. But he said nothing. He just took her hand and pulled her up the trail.

The hike was long and silent. Taylor felt as if the world outside this forest had ceased to exist. There was just her and Seth and the water that streamed from the skies. When she had decided they'd have to walk forever to get back, the lighted windows of the lodge beamed through the rain, guiding them home.

And this was *home*. That realization came to Taylor with clear, crystallized certainty.

Seth had brought her home.

Chapter Six

"... When he kisses me I can't think. Sometimes I want to run from him. Or maybe from myself. The only thing I know for sure is that I want him to kiss me again...."

Until tonight, Taylor hadn't felt the lodge's lack of privacy. She liked Millie and the rest of the staff. She loved being with her grandfather and with Josh. She even enjoyed talking with the guests at meals or in the evenings. Tonight, however, the only person she wanted to see was Seth. But he had disappeared.

When they had reached the lodge after their hike, he left her standing in the rain. Without speaking, he just walked off. She started to follow him, to force a confrontation about what had happened. But Gerald had spotted her from the porch, so there was nothing to do but go to the cabin, shower and get into clean, dry clothes.

Afterward, she went up to the lodge for a late dinner. Gerald wanted to know all about the hike. She told him about the bear, and soon she had to recount the story to everyone on the premises. Ten o'clock arrived before she was able to make her excuses and go in search of Seth.

There were lights in his cabin, and from the half-opened windows came music, mingling with the sound of rain hitting the porch's tin roof. Taylor stood at the bottom of the steps, listening. The acoustic melody and soaring harmonies were familiar, a folk rock hit from over twenty years ago; it had been one of her mother's favorites. Taylor had grown up listening to this music. Feeling as if the tune was a good omen, she mounted the steps and knocked on the door.

Seth was slow to respond, but he didn't look surprised to see her when he opened the door. Silently, he stepped aside and allowed her to enter.

He said nothing as she shed her rain slicker and hung it on a peg beside the door. The music played on, an odd, cheerful counterpoint to the tension in the room.

Taylor finally broke the impasse. "I hope you got something to eat."

"Millie brought some soup over."

"That's good. It's cold and wet out." As if to illustrate the obvious, a sodden, chilly breeze blew through the windows. Taylor shivered, rubbing her hands on her sweatered arms. "Aren't you freezing?"

"There's a fire."

For the first time, she noticed the roaring blaze across the room. The stone fireplace was larger than the one in Gerald's cabin, dominating one entire wall. "Your heat's going out the windows."

"I like it this way." He turned on his heel and crossed the room, leaving her to frown after him. In a dark blue sweater and gray corduroy pants, he loomed larger and more unapproachable than ever before. Especially with his shoulders held so straight and rigid.

"Josh is up at the lodge," she offered unnecessarily. "Playing Scrabble with some of the guests."

Not looking up, he added a log to the fire. "I know."

She swallowed. "Since he's not here, I thought—"

Seth's head jerked up. "What?"

"We could talk," she completed. "What did you think I was going to say?"

Shaking his head, he replaced the fireplace screen. "Nothing."

"You do agree we need to talk, don't you?"

He turned his back to the fireplace and rubbed a hand over his face, looking weary. "I don't know what there is to say."

"You think we should just let it go?"

He hesitated, then nodded.

"I don't know about you, but I can't pretend it didn't happen."

"Why not?" His gaze met hers then, almost in challenge.

"Because I don't kiss people like that as just a matter of course."

"Let's not make more of it than what it was. It was just an impulse." He spread his hands wide. "Just one of those things."

Some other woman might have agreed with him, donned her coat and gone off to nurse her wounded pride in private. But it had never been Taylor's style to back down when she thought she was right. She lifted her chin. "It felt like more than 'one of those things' to me."

"Taylor, come on...."

"No, you come on. Tell me why you kissed me."

The direct question made him flinch. A muscle twitched over his eye as he answered. "Meeting up with that bear was pretty unnerving. Of course, if I hadn't been preoccupied, it wouldn't have happened, and I'm sorry—"

"Why were you preoccupied?"

"I just was, okay?" he retorted impatiently. "But the point is, you were frightened. Then we had a hard time getting down the mountain. And I...I kissed you because..." He paused, looked at her, then away. "It just happened. That's all there is to it."

She stepped forward, her hands falling to the back of a rocking chair for support. "And that's that, huh?"

He nodded.

"You're lying."

"Taylor, come on, let's just drop it."

"I don't want to drop it." She gripped the chair's smooth wood, needing something tangible to bolster her courage. Finally, she took a deep breath and spoke straight from her heart. "I wanted you to kiss me. I've wanted it for days now."

Though Seth knew she was being honest, he didn't want to hear it. He still couldn't believe he had lost his grip so completely today. But when she had turned to him, her eyes wide and frightened, with the rain streaming over her, he had acted on impulse. Pure impulse.

"You've wanted the same thing."

Her quiet words startled him into a denial. "You don't know that."

"But I do."

"Listen," he cut in, fumbling for explanations. "I'll admit there's been something brewing between us, but—"

She cocked an eyebrow. "Just some*thing?*"

"Maybe it has to do with Gerald. I've had a hard time adjusting to the thought of losing him. You've been emotional, too. We've argued. Feelings have run high since you got here. I don't really know what's happened—"

"Surely a man your age *knows* what's happening."

That needled him. "A man my age should *know* better than to become entangled with a woman your age."

She left the chair rocking as she crossed the room. "So you admit that we're becoming entangled?"

Realizing he was trapped, Seth turned away. He shoved his hands into his pockets and stared down at the fire. He didn't look up, not even when Taylor touched his arm.

"Tell me I'm not crazy," she murmured. "Tell me what happened today was incredible."

He closed his eyes. Yet he couldn't close his mind. He couldn't block out those moments in the rain, with Taylor like a wild creature in his arms. He had wanted to lay her down, to make her his. On the wet ground. With the wind whipping the trees. And the rain beating on their skin. When he thought of that impulse, it seemed impossible that they should be standing here now, discussing it in such civilized tones. You couldn't cage such explosive passion. You couldn't deny it, either.

So he looked up at her, and he left off the senseless denials. "You're not crazy."

Her answering smile was the sort that inspired dreams.

Hesitantly, feeling like a kid who had never touched a woman, he put a hand to her cheek. Her skin was as smooth as he remembered. Without a thought for what he was doing, his fingertips feathered along her jaw. He stroked his thumb across her lips. Once. Twice. Till the ache in his heart became unbearable.

He put his arms around her, but he didn't kiss her again. It seemed far more important just to hold her. With Taylor in his arms, he didn't have to imagine her scent. He could allow himself the luxury of rubbing his cheek against her hair and taking long breaths of her sweet fragrance. There was so much to savor. The rhythm of her breathing. The gentle thrust of her breasts against his chest. The nubby texture of her sweater beneath his hands. The movement of her thighs against his own.

He didn't know how long they stood, just holding each other. It could have gone on forever, as far as he was concerned. There was nothing else either of them should be doing at this moment. Outside, the rain still fell. Behind them, the fire crackled. And from the stereo came a mellow classic about teaching your children well.

"I know this song," Taylor whispered.

"I'm not sure you were born when they recorded this."

"Mom loved it," she continued in a dreamy tone. "Before we met my stepfather, Mom and I lived in this little one-room apartment. She had this old record player and about a dozen albums that she played over and over. The neighbors complained and the landlady threatened to throw us out. She didn't, though."

"Maybe she learned to appreciate good music."

Taylor laughed. "I think she just felt sorry for us. Mother was broke most of the time. The heat kept getting cut off. And it was so cold. I can remember the snow falling outside the window and this music playing while Mother danced me around the room. We stayed warm, dancing. And ever since, each time I hear this song, I feel safe."

The picture she painted was so vivid he could see Taylor, a little girl with brown-gold hair and big eyes, laughing up into her mother's face. Seth had spared few charitable thoughts for Holly Austin Cantrell, but he knew what it was like to be alone with the responsibility for a child. If it was hard for him, with Gerald and Millie to help, he could only imagine what it must have been like for Holly, so young and alone in a strange, cold city. No matter what else Holly had done, she had managed to raise this daughter. This strong, beautiful woman whom he held so tightly.

Taylor tipped her face up to his. "You know what? I feel safe right now."

Emotion roughened his voice. "You shouldn't."

"Why?"

"Because at the moment I'm not feeling very cautious."

"That's fine with me."

He kissed her then. He claimed her mouth with a greed he hadn't known he possessed. She matched his fervor, and his body hardened in response to the demands she made.

Some lingering trace of sanity made him break away before matters got completely out of hand. "Damn, Taylor. I don't know what I'm doing."

Her laughter was soft. "You're faking it awfully well, then."

He held her away. "Be serious. You're closer to my son's age than mine."

"So?"

"And you're Gerald's granddaughter."

"What does that matter?"

"When you were three years old, dancing in a freezing apartment with your mother, I was on the crew of a plane flying cargo missions over the jungle. This song has always reminded me of guns."

Taylor blinked. "And what possible impact does that have on this moment?"

"It's just that I'm not a kid."

"Neither am I. Or hadn't you noticed?"

He had noticed. How he had noticed.

They came together again. Somehow, they made it to the couch. Soon, it was obvious that kisses wouldn't be nearly enough. Taylor told him it wasn't enough. Seth's hand was on the front clasp of her bra when they heard the footsteps on the porch steps. There was barely time to spring apart before Josh burst into the room.

He stopped, mouth dropping open, as if the sight of his father and Taylor sitting side by side on the couch was the shock of his young life. No one said a word.

Taylor smoothed her hair into place. Seth got up to stoke the fire again. He was happy to keep his back to the room until he could get his body and his mind under control.

Frantically, Taylor searched for something to break the tension in the room. "How was Scrabble?" It was an inane question, but the best she could come up with under the circumstances.

Still looking startled, Josh mumbled a reply. He sprawled in the chair closest to the couch.

She swallowed and attempted an explanation to his unspoken question. "I just dropped in to talk to Se— to your father for a minute."

Josh frowned. "Gerald said you went to bed."

"I guess I was . . . uh . . . too keyed up from today. With what happened with the bear . . . and everything else . . ." *Lord, but she was making a mess of this. Why didn't Seth say something?*

As if in reply to her unspoken plea, he finally turned from the fire. His smile had an artificial look to it. "Yeah . . . well, the bear was something."

Since Josh was looking at them both like they were lunatics, Taylor thought it time to cut their losses and run. She sprang to her feet. "I've got to go."

Seth moved just as fast. "I've got a few things to check on, too."

They had seized their slickers and plunged out of the cabin before Josh could protest again. When the cabin was safely out of sight, Seth took her arm and drew her into the shelter of some trees. "This is too complicated."

Perhaps the subterfuge made her bold. "I want you," she whispered. "There's nothing complicated about that." And her lips lifted to his.

Groaning, he kissed her again. But a kiss was all he gave.

"Go home," he said. "It's cold and wet. Gerald's probably worried about you. And I've got to go face my son, who has the hots for you, himself."

"That's not true—"

"Don't be so sure. You were never a sixteen-year-old boy with raging hormones."

"No, I'm twenty-five, and something *is* raging. I don't want to go—"

He set her away from him. "Just where could we go, Taylor? Can you tell me where we could go to be alone?" To prove his point, they heard the laughter of a group of guests who were coming from the lodge to their cabins.

"Tomorrow," Taylor promised before striking off toward Gerald's cabin.

Her grandfather was waiting beside the fire, as usual. She told him she had gone for a walk. If he saw anything suspicious in Taylor's expression or manner, he didn't comment. Truthfully, she didn't think she had done anything of which he would disapprove. He loved Seth like a son. He trusted him even more. But she didn't confide in Gerald. What was

happening between her and Seth was too new, too unsettling to share with anyone just yet.

She kissed Gerald good-night and went to bed,
looking forward to tomorrow.

Tomorrow.

Her head was on the pillow before she realized Seth
hadn't promised anything about tomorrow.

Muttering an impatient oath to himself, Seth strode
through the lodge's main hall and banged open the
door of a small, cedar-paneled office. One of the
young male employees looked up from the desk with
a startled expression.

"Sorry, Randy," Seth muttered. "I'm looking for
Josh."

"I think he took Taylor fishing."

"Only Taylor?"

"Yes, sir."

"Great, just great." Seth pushed a hand through his
hair. *Confound the boy, anyway. He had lost his head
this past week.*

"Anything I can do?" Randy asked.

Seth managed a short laugh. "I know it's your day
off, but do you feel like taking a couple of guests on a
hike up to the lake? Josh promised them he would do
it, but I guess he forgot."

The young man, who had worked for the lodge
three summers in a row, nodded. "No problem, boss.
I was just checking the schedule to see if I could hitch

a ride into Juneau, but I'd much rather earn some overtime pay.''

''Thanks. The guests are waiting out front.''

When Randy had departed, Seth took a seat at the desk. He flipped on the computer, but then merely glared at the screen. He didn't know what had gotten into Josh these past few days.

But that wasn't really true. Josh had been on his worst behavior ever since he had surprised Seth and Taylor in the cabin. The boy had said nothing, but Seth knew he had his suspicions. Why else had he been sticking so close to Taylor's side? He had been surly with Seth, had forgotten promises to guests, had left chores undone.

Wheeling his chair around to face the window, Seth blew out an exasperated breath. It was comical, really, having to compete with his son for Taylor's time. Not that Seth had competed very hard. He and Josh had enough problems without a woman coming between them, too. He didn't believe Taylor was encouraging Josh's puppy love, but the boy was hard to shake when he dug in his heels. Josh had decided to take over the job of showing her the area. Wearing a rather helpless look on her face, she had been pulled off on hikes, trips to Juneau and flights over the glaciers.

Seth wasn't happy about Josh neglecting the guests, but on the other hand, he was almost glad his son was taking up Taylor's time. It gave Seth a chance to step back, to think about what he was getting himself into.

It wasn't that he didn't crave the sweetness Taylor offered. He had almost lost control that night in his cabin. But the possible complications were mind-boggling.

Complications. In Seth's life, there had been plenty of them. Especially when a woman was involved.

At eighteen, he had been hopelessly, foolishly in love with the prettiest girl in his senior class. Together, they had explored those first, aching rites of passion. He could still remember how beautiful she had been. Honey-gold hair. Big blue eyes. Pale-as-moonlight skin. Her parents had thought him reckless and discouraged her.

He joined the air force. She promised to wait. But a month into his Vietnam tour, she wrote to say she was marrying someone else—a big-time rancher's son with money in the bank and an educational deferment that would keep him out of stinking, rotting jungles.

On his first leave, Seth had blown all his pay on a prostitute in Saigon. They spent the weekend together. Then he started a bar brawl with a fellow officer whose only crime was calling the woman what she was. Seth was lucky to escape disciplinary action.

He managed to avoid feminine complications for a while. Once he was stateside, he even dated some nice girls. One of them was Josh's mother.

Then she turned out to have the heart of a viper.

While he no longer thought the same of Taylor, he felt he had reason to exercise caution before they got in any deeper. He had to think about the long-range consequences. In three or four weeks, she was scheduled to leave, to go back to the city she spoke of with such love. Back to her real life.

He knew that Gerald had the idea that Taylor might decide she wanted to stay here. Seth held out no such hopes. She would go home, eventually. And she would wonder why she had lost her head over a man like him.

Seth had been tossed aside plenty of times in his life. One more instance shouldn't matter. But it did. He didn't know why, but he didn't want Taylor going back to Chicago and regretting a relationship with him.

He didn't like admitting it, but maybe, just like Gerald, he wanted her to care. About this land. About the lodge. But most of all, about him. She said she wanted him. But that was only sex. Seth knew how fast sex could burn itself out. With someone other than Taylor it might be enough. But she made him want so much more.

So much.

"Is this a private party, or can I come in?"

Swiveling from the window, Seth found Millie standing in the doorway. He smiled at his friend. "You can always come in."

Today the older woman's ever-present apron was a bright blue. It almost matched her eyes. Even though they twinkled, she groaned as she took the chair opposite Seth's desk.

"Busy morning?" he asked in sympathy.

"No more than usual. I'm just getting old."

"Impossible. You'll always be twenty-one, Millie-girl."

"My old bones say otherwise."

His chair squeaked as Seth leaned forward and sighed. "I guess we all have to face it."

Her tone assumed its customary crispness. "I'll have none of that from you."

He looked up in surprise. "You're always telling me I'm getting old, too."

"But I don't mean it."

"It's true, though."

Gray hair danced around her face as she shook her head. "You're still young, Seth. You've got half your life in front of you."

"Not half, surely."

"Why not? You're strong and healthy."

"Gerald was, too, at my age."

"Well, I'll give you that," she agreed. "He was so strong and so healthy that all he did was work. For too many years, he spent all his time trying not to think about Holly. Even after you and the boy came, he worked on. He worked and grieved himself right into that first heart attack." Sadness darkened her eyes. "The things he did to forget . . . that's what destroyed his health."

She was right, of course. Millie was rarely wrong about those she loved. And she did love Gerald. All these years, Seth had sat back, wondering if Gerald knew how much Millie cared. Gerald treated her with gentle affection, but Seth wasn't sure if he truly appreciated all the small things Millie did to make his life more comfortable. He wished Gerald could have loved this woman. With her easy laugh and tough-tender ways, she had added a great deal to all of their lives. She could have done more if Gerald had only opened his eyes. Or his heart.

Millie shifted in her chair, fixing Seth with the steady gaze he knew only too well. "I'm going to prevail upon our friendship, Seth."

He chuckled. "Since when have you not?"

"No jokes," she said solemnly. "I'm giving you some advice." She took the breath that always preceeded one of her pronouncements. "Don't end up like Gerald. Or me."

He dropped his gaze to the desk, suddenly sure he didn't want to hear what Millie was about to say. "Oh, now, Millie—"

"I mean it, now," she continued, her voice gruff. "When I came to this lodge, I was in pain, just like you were. My husband had died in a logging accident. Before him, I had put two babies in the ground, and the Lord hadn't blessed me with any more. I felt pretty beaten down. Then I came here and found Gerald, who was in a sorrier state than me. And in those first years..." Her eyes grew suspiciously moist. "Well, let's just say things could have been different if I had pushed the case a little harder. I didn't, and that's what I live with. But you don't have to."

Seth shuffled some papers on the desk, uncomfortable with the woman's revelations, not certain what she was driving at.

She stood then, arms akimbo, practically forcing him to look at her. "I'm not saying my life's been bad. I've had a world of joy. I even got to do some mothering—to Josh. If I never say it again, I want you to know I'm grateful to you for that, Seth."

He nodded, not trusting himself to speak.

Millie laughed softly. "It's funny, isn't it? You and me and Gerald—three broken souls—raising that boy. But we've done a fair job of it, I think."

Seth found his voice. "There's still a bit to do."

But Millie shook her head. "Not much. And soon Josh is going to leave."

Though it was only the truth, Seth didn't want to hear anyone else say it. "Maybe not...."

"Yes, he will leave," Millie insisted. "And then what about you?"

He frowned. "I'll just be here—working. This is my home, after all."

"That's what I'm afraid of. I don't want you here, alone, growing older. Colder."

He frowned at the last word. "Millie, I think you've made your point, okay?"

"No, I haven't, because I've not yet mentioned Taylor."

That shocked him. "What about Taylor?"

Millie clucked. "I have eyes, Seth. Lord, a person doesn't need eyes when you two are in the same room. I can feel what's going on."

"There is nothing going on," Seth countered in measured tones.

"Gerald says—"

"Gerald?" The blood drained from Seth's face. "What about Gerald?"

"Oh, settle down, now. Gerald's no fool, and he has eyes, too. And nothing would make him happier than you and Taylor."

"There is no me and Taylor." The moment the words were out, Seth thought of what had passed between them in the rain and in his cabin. He thought of all he had contemplated with Taylor, and a guilty flush heated his cheeks.

Millie cackled with laughter. "You never have been much of a liar."

He settled back in his chair, feeling as if all the wind had been kicked from his lungs. *Gerald and Millie discussing him and Taylor? And here he thought Josh was the only one who suspected.*

Millie's voice roused him from his state of shock. "You need Taylor," she said bluntly. "You may not even realize how much. But I want you to realize it before it's too late."

She left him no chance to reply. In a swirl of bright blue apron, she was gone, leaving Seth to gape after her in consternation.

But dull anger followed close on the heels of her departure. So Millie thought he *needed* Taylor? That was crazy. He hadn't needed a woman for more than momentary pleasure in a long, long time. Taylor might make him yearn for some unnameable, intangible connection. But he was smart enough to know it would never come to be.

He started to get up from his chair, intending to tell Millie he didn't appreciate her sticking her nose in his personal business. But he reined in his temper quickly. He had learned long ago that it was no use arguing with the woman when she made up her mind about something. In fact, she liked a good fight. He wasn't going to give her the satisfaction. He would ignore her.

Growling to himself about busybodies, he turned back to his computer. But no amount of banging on the keyboard helped erase Millie's words.

So she knew Josh's growing up was getting to him.

She feared Seth would become a cold and lonely old man.

She thought Taylor was the answer.

Taylor.

Taylor wasn't an answer. She was the question—a great, big "what if" in the middle of his life. What if he stopped hesitating? What if he followed the crazy impulse that had seized them the other night? What if...

He shut off the computer with a little snap of the switch, wishing his brain would shut down as quickly. Then he stomped through the lodge, ignoring the curious stares of the few guests who were lounging about in the hall.

Gerald was on the front porch, enjoying the rare sunshine. "What's your hurry?" he asked as Seth passed.

"I'm going flying," Seth answered, not even pausing as he took the front steps two at a time. He usually had all the time in the world for Gerald, but he wasn't sure he could look his friend in the eyes with the question of Taylor hanging between them.

On the way to the dock, an employee stopped to ask him a question. Seth sent her to Millie. Let the woman take care of everything. She was so sure she knew what was right for them all—let her run the lodge. Seth didn't care if everyone in the place needed him this morning. He had to get away.

But of course Josh and Taylor had taken the smallest plane, Seth's favorite. Seth was left with one of the larger craft, a massive waste of fuel for one person. Despite that, he took it and flew for hours—over mountains, glaciers and islands. To assuage his guilt over the amount of time he had spent away from the business, he stopped in Juneau, checking in at the office and refueling before he started the return flight to the lodge.

Flying could usually calm Seth. There was something soothing and peaceful about soaring high above the Earth. But the trick didn't work today. Today he just got angrier and angrier.

Taylor. She was at the root of every problem. *Taylor*—with her bewitching smile and innocent eyes. *Taylor*—who reminded him more sharply than anyone else of the empty holes in his life.

Though she had done a world of good for Gerald, Seth wished with all his heart that she had never come here. His life, which had already been confused enough, was worse now. Right at this moment, she was probably talking to Josh, filling the boy's head with thoughts of leaving home. Seth was putting a stop to that today. No, he wasn't foolish or selfish enough to think he could keep the boy here forever. In a couple of years, Josh could go anywhere he wanted. But right now he was sixteen and he was staying home where he belonged.

Filled with resolve, Seth brought the plane down onto the river. A line of floatplanes bobbed at the dock. Pilots were loading a group of cruise passengers who had flown over for a grilled salmon lunch. Seth's anger burned anew as he realized the smaller craft Josh had taken was nowhere in sight.

"Anybody heard from Josh?" he asked each of the pilots in turn.

At their negative responses, Seth tried calling Josh on his plane's radio. There was no answer. He headed for the lodge. Millie met him at the door, a worried look on her face.

"I've tried rousing him by radio since about one," she said, following him to the office. "He told me before he left this morning that he would be back at noon. He was taking her to that stream where you and Gerald have always fished. They should have been back, Seth.''

Worry began to edge past Seth's anger.

Gerald appeared in the doorway, his brow knitting as he directed a glance from Millie to Seth. ''What's wrong?''

Seth didn't want him upset, so he managed a slight laugh. ''Josh has decided his only responsibility is to show Taylor around. He took her fishing, evidently for the whole day. They've probably tapped into a good run of salmon and lost track of time.''

''Hasn't he called in?''

They had a rule at the lodge. Anytime one of them took a plane out to the more remote areas, they radioed in periodically. Either Josh had chosen to ignore the rule, or he was in trouble. He and Taylor.

But Seth couldn't dwell on that possibility. ''It's no big deal,'' he said for Gerald's benefit. ''I'm sure they're just having a good time and we'll see the plane come in soon.''

Two hours later, there was still no Josh, no Taylor and no radio contact. Gerald was pacing back and forth on the porch. Millie had burned two pies and been pushed out of her own kitchen by her helpers. Seth felt like one long, ragged nerve.

He was on his way to the dock, ready to mount a search, when Josh's plane appeared, skimming low over the river, making a perfect landing. That was a good sign, but still, Seth broke into a run.

Josh was the first out of the plane, grinning blithely, turning to help Taylor. Her smile widened as she stepped onto the dock and looked at Seth, who slid to a halt nearby. "This is quite a reception," she said, her eyes dancing with mischief. "Miss me?"

Seth was so damn glad to see they were both safe that he said nothing for minute. Then the anger set in again. "Where have you been?"

Taylor's smile disappeared. "We were fishing. But what's…" She pressed a hand to her throat. "There's nothing wrong, is there? Gerald—"

"Gerald is fine," Seth cut in coldly. As Josh started to pass, he caught him by the sleeve of his jacket. "Now suppose you tell me where you've been all day?"

The boy jerked away. "Taylor told you. We were fishing."

"You were supposed to be back at noon."

"We were delayed."

"And you couldn't answer your radio?"

"It's busted."

"Busted?" Seth repeated. "Was it busted when you left?"

Josh's insolent shrug was the only answer Seth needed.

"How could you do that?" he demanded. "You never go out without a radio. You've known that since you were ten years old."

"And you're the one who's supposed to keep the radios working," Josh shot back. He cut his eyes toward Taylor. "Except maybe radios aren't what's on your mind these days."

Taylor stepped forward. "Josh, don't—"

Seth caught his arm again. "Why don't you come out and say what's bothering you, son?"

Josh glared at him. "You bother me, Dad. Just you."

"I'm not the one who stayed gone all day long, who worried everyone to death."

"You don't *have* to worry about me. I can take care of myself."

"Obviously not. Or you wouldn't have pulled this crazy stunt."

"Seth," Taylor interrupted. "Maybe it was my fault. Josh was showing me—"

Seth cut her off. "Stay out of this."

"But, Seth—"

"I said, stay out of it," he said, his voice rising.

Josh swore at him, once again jerking his arm out of Seth's grasp. "Don't yell at her. You can treat me like a baby and order me around like a slave, but don't yell at her."

"I think you've said enough," Seth said, struggling to keep his tone even. "Now go to the cabin."

"Sure, Dad, I'll go." Josh turned and ran down the dock, but not without a few last, angry words. "I can't wait till I can go away from here forever."

Taylor winced at the words. Her mother had written the same phrase in her diary twenty-six years ago. No doubt, she had flung them at Gerald, too.

She caught hold of Seth's arms. "You've got to go after him."

He shook her off. Eyes blazing, face set in harsh lines, he glared at her. "Don't tell me what to do with my son."

"Seth, he's so confused. He needs someone to talk to—"

"Well, it's not you. From now on, I want you to stay away from him."

Then he was gone, striding down the path opposite the one his son had chosen.

Why? Taylor wondered. *Why would he tempt history into repeating itself?*

Chapter Seven

"...I wish someone had told me love was so frightening. Is it like this for everyone? For Mom and Dad? I doubt it. I wish there was someone who could tell me the way I should feel..."

The summer night fell at the lodge with only a subtle darkening of the sky. For the first time since she had arrived, Taylor wished for a true nightfall. After this afternoon's ugly clash between Seth and Josh, there was something singularly appealing about the cover of darkness. Then the sun would seem all the brighter tomorrow. Maybe everything would seem brighter.

Tonight was also the first time she had felt the remoteness of the lodge. They were connected to the outside world only by radio. If she had followed her earlier impulse, she could have flown into Juneau with the evening's last load of cruise passengers. She could have gotten a hotel room, made a long-distance phone call and flown back here tomorrow, no doubt fortified by some of Joe's wisdom.

But the floatplanes full of tourists were gone, and she hadn't moved from her seat in the rocking chair on the porch of Gerald's cabin.

What would Joe tell me?

The question made her smile. Joe wasn't given to advice. He was a psychologist who believed in making people find the answers to their problems within themselves. He had applied the same theories to child rearing. Ever since she was a little girl, he had turned most of her questions around. *"What do you think, Taylor? Do you think that's the right way to behave?"*

Her mother had always said Taylor was born old, but perhaps it was those first, struggling years, when they were alone together, that had forced a grown-up maturity on her. Or maybe the maturity stemmed from Joe's gentle insistence that she think for herself. For whatever the reason, Taylor applied logic to most of the situations that confronted her. She wasn't given to the impulsiveness which plagued many of her friends.

But Seth Hardy made her reckless.

The sane and sensible part of Taylor's brain told her she should forget about him. He was much too hard. Life had dealt him too many blows. But the other part of her, the part that was intrigued by his tantalizing flashes of tenderness, told her to hang in there. Better yet, the reckless side of her told her to run to him, take every chance in the world to win him.

She had never behaved like this, never thrown herself at anyone, never awakened in the middle of the night gasping from dark, sensual dreams of one, certain man. Seth Hardy had turned her world around.

He gave her no encouragement. He had accused her of being a fortune hunter. He said a relationship between them was too complicated. He thought she was encouraging his son into disobedience. He kissed her and made no promises. Even if he made love to her, she knew there would be no guarantees about tomorrow. She was probably being very foolish. And yet she wanted to go to him now, to put her hand in his, to lay her head on his shoulder and look up at the bright sky.

Footsteps sounded along the path from the lodge, and Taylor sat up, hoping against hope that Seth was coming to talk. But it was Gerald who appeared among the trees. The bouyance that had marked his step in recent days was gone.

Concerned, she surveyed his stooped shoulders. "It's late. I was wondering when you were coming in."

He climbed the porch steps with a heavy sigh. "I've been talking to Josh."

"Is he okay?"

"Oh, he's licking his wounds and plotting revenge. He has the usual complaints. His father treats him like a child. He's tired of living in this backwater. He wants to go live with some friends in Juneau."

"Does he really think his father would just let him go away like that?"

Gerald dropped into the chair beside hers, looking weary. "Maybe Seth should go himself."

She thought of the look on Seth's face when he had called this valley his home. "How could he leave? He loves it here."

"He could run the lodge just as well from Juneau, and Josh would be happier. Maybe that's what I should have done. Holly might have stayed."

Taylor shook her head. "Mother left because she was in love. Sure, the two of you argued, but it wasn't the lodge she was running from. She loved it here."

Gerald closed his eyes. "That's a wonderful thought, Taylor, but we'll never know if it's really true, will we?"

"It's in her diary."

He hesitated, then said softly, "I'd like to read that diary, Taylor."

She had wondered when this request would come. "Some of what she wrote will hurt you."

"Not any more than her leaving."

"Or her refusal to forgive you when you found her?"

He sucked in his breath. "How do you know about that?"

She had been waiting for the right time to ask Gerald about the trip he had made to Chicago. This moment was as right as any would ever be. "Seth told me."

"I should have expected he would."

Taylor went on to explain all she knew about Gerald's visit to Holly. He filled in the blank spaces, telling her about the private investigator he hired to track her down, about the cold, spring morning when he had arrived at her door.

"She wouldn't let me in the house," Gerald whispered. "We just stood on the porch. She looked so grown-up. And she was still so angry with me. She told me she hated me."

Taylor reached for his hand.

"Until that moment I would never have believed my Holly could hate me so much. All I ever wanted to do was protect her." He had to clear his throat in order to continue. "I handled it badly from the beginning. I refused to see what was happening that summer. She was seventeen and I treated her like she was seven. When she came to me, told me about her and...and well, told me she was pregnant, I was so hurt. I felt so betrayed."

"And maybe that's the real reason she pushed you away," Taylor murmured. Her mother's refusal to forgive Gerald hadn't made sense to her until now. "Maybe she didn't want to face how she had hurt you. Maybe it was easier for her to keep on pretending she hated you."

"Perhaps you're right," Gerald said. "But when I think of all you and she must have gone through at first... it's the most abject failure of my life. In the end, I couldn't protect my own family."

Taylor was silent, feeling his renewed anguish. How could Seth risk this sort of estrangement with Josh? All he really had to do was stop holding Josh on such a tight rein and start listening to the boy's plans and dreams.

She looked at Gerald. "You and Seth are so much alike, you know, wanting so desperately to protect what's your own."

"Like wolves guarding our family packs," Gerald muttered.

She was struck by his comparison. So many times Seth had made her think of a wolf. Proud and alone. Watching the world from a shadowed vantage point.

Gerald sighed. "I don't want Seth and Josh to go through what Holly and I did."

"You don't think Josh would really run away, do you?"

"I didn't think Holly would, and look what happened."

Exasperation sent her to her feet. "Seth has to do something. He's got to change the way he approaches Josh."

"Admitting that your child is growing up and away from you is hard, especially when that child is all you have."

"You've got to talk to him."

"I have." Gerald paused, sending a shrewd glance her way. "Perhaps you're the one who can help Seth."

Taylor could tell from that look that her grandfather was not unaware of the undercurrents between her and Seth. She was glad. She had nothing to hide. So she straightened her shoulders and returned his steady regard. "I would like to help Seth, but in order for that to happen, he has to let me in. He has to get rid of the Off-Limits sign."

"And you have to understand he hasn't known much tenderness."

"I know about his childhood."

"It's more than that. Seth doesn't know the way it can be when two people really care for one another. I think he is one of the finest individuals it has ever been my privilege to know. He's been a good friend. But I don't pretend he's easy to understand. You have to work at getting close to him."

"That's for certain."

Gerald hesitated again, then pressed on. "I don't want to pry, Taylor. You can tell me this is none of my business. But are you sure you want to be involved with Seth? You've known him for only a few weeks and . . . well, I guess what I'm trying to ask is what do you really feel for him?"

Instead of giving her first, instinctive answer, she went to the porch railing. She tipped her head back and searched the bright, Alaskan night for an explanation.

What did she feel for Seth? What words could she use to describe the wild exhilaration she felt in his arms? Was there a phrase for the awful tenderness that engulfed her when he talked of his love for this land? Could she put a name to the emotions that bloomed inside her when he looked at Gerald, smiled at Josh or teased Millie?

In the end, she went with her instincts. "I think I'm falling in love with him."

Gerald was silent.

She faced him, wanting his opinion, his approval. "What do you think?"

His words sounded as if they were carefully chosen. "Loving Seth Hardy will be a challenge. It might be a little like your grandmother loving me. I didn't make it easy on Sarah. I took her away from her home. I forced her into a new and strange land."

"She went willingly, I think. And it sounds to me like you made a wonderful life together."

Gerald sighed. "Yes, that we did." Then he looked at Taylor again, a worried frown wrinkling his brow. "Don't let Seth hurt you, Taylor. Please."

Taylor promised she wouldn't, though she knew her words were worth little. She feared Seth had the capacity to bring her both incredible joy and unspeakable sadness.

She went inside with her grandfather and gave him the diary, but somehow it seemed an intrusion to stay while he began to read Holly's words. Taylor left him alone and went in search of Seth.

* * *

He had known she would come. All evening long, working in the machine shed to repair the broken radio from the plane, Seth had waited for Taylor. He wasn't surprised when, not long after ten o'clock, she appeared in the doorway.

He looked up from the worktable, gazed into her strangely defiant green-gold eyes, then turned back to his work.

She came inside. "I think we should talk."

"I don't think there's much to say." Carefully he fitted the radio's back panel in place.

"I feel responsible for what happened today."

"I'm sure you didn't know to question Josh about the radio. He's the one who broke one of our hard and fast rules. He knew better than to take off without any way to call for help."

Without invitation, she perched on one of the stools opposite him. The harsh glare of the single bulb that hung over the worktable cast shadows on her pale, earnest face. But not even that ugly light could take away from the smoothness of her skin, the bright beauty of her eyes. The shed smelled of motor oil and grease, but she made it seem almost pleasant.

Seth looked away, trying to concentrate on his work, determined not to unbend, not to let her get to him.

"I'm the reason Josh stayed so long up at the stream," she insisted. "It was so beautiful there, with the water tumbling down the rocks and the salmon jumping. I tried to sketch it while Josh fished. We saw another bear, too, but it stayed away.''

"And what if it hadn't?'' Seth demanded. "What if Josh or you had slipped on one of those rocks and fallen? The plane was what—two, maybe three miles away, down on the river? Think how long it would have taken to get to the plane, and then, without a radio, think how much longer it would have taken to get help.''

"That's not what happened.''

"But it could have.'' The thought of all that could have happened still made him angry. "I know here at the lodge we seem pretty civilized, but out there it's still wilderness.''

"That's what I love about it.''

"You don't know it well enough to love it.''

Her lips tightened. "You're wrong.''

Shrugging, he continued, "Regardless of your romantic notions, this isn't a land where you take chances. I've taught Josh the right way to take care of himself from the day I brought him here. So I'm very disappointed by what he did today. He put you both in danger.''

Taylor's eyes narrowed. "And you won't let him forget it, will you?''

Seth glared at her. "I thought I made it clear today that what happens between me and my son is none of your business.''

"But I want to help.''

"Then just stay out of it.''

She regarded him in silence for a moment. "That's what you want me to do, isn't it? You wish I would just turn around, walk out that door and leave you alone. That would make it easy for you to keep on believing you don't need anyone."

In the space of just one day, both Taylor and Millie had spoken of his needs, as if they had all the answers. How could they be so certain of what he doubted? Seth straightened from his stool and began packing his tools away. He didn't want to think about his needs. He was determined not to have another confrontation with Taylor.

"That's very good," she said after several moments had passed. "Just ignore me and maybe I'll fade away. Maybe if you ignore your real problem with Josh, it'll go away, too."

He closed the lid of his tool chest, unable to resist indulging in some sarcasm. "Since you seem to be such an expert on the subject, just what is my real problem with Josh?"

"You're just so damn scared of him growing up and leaving you alone."

He forced himself to laugh. "You and Millie should get together and compare notes."

"So this isn't a new concept I'm talking about."

"The concept—yours and Millie's—is full of it," Seth said in blunt finality. "My problem with Josh is that he thinks he's grown-up right now. And he's not. But maybe, if people like you would stop encouraging him to rebel, he would settle down."

Taylor's voice rose to match his. "I haven't encouraged Josh to do anything. All I do is listen to his dreams. Gerald does the same. So does Millie. But you're the most important person in his life. If you would listen to him, talk to him instead of barking orders, maybe he wouldn't feel as if he's in a prison."

Anger simmering now, Seth stepped toward her. "How do you know whether I talk to Josh? What is it, after less than a month here, that makes you an expert on what's best for me and my son?"

"It's not just me. Obviously Gerald and Millie think you should cut him some slack, too."

"Despite how much I care for Millie and Gerald, in the last estimation Josh is my son, my responsibility. *Mine.*"

Taylor flung her head back, the defiance burning brighter in her gaze. "He's yours, all right. There's not a person who would deny that. He's full of pride. He's obstinate as hell. And he would rather cut off his arm than reveal the slightest weakness. You've definitely raised a son cut from your own image."

Her words startled Seth. Other than superficial comparisons, he had never thought of Josh as being so much like him.

Taylor slid from her stool, her voice softening. "Remember the day at the lake? You told me that when you were a teenager, all you wanted to do was fly right out of the town where you grew up. You weren't unique, you know. Just about everyone I've ever known has wanted to do the same. Josh isn't any different. He's full of big talk. And being your son, he's more impatient than most. The biggest mistake you could make would be turning a simple case of teenage rebellion into something more.''

While her words made sense, Seth wasn't ready to admit she was right. ''Josh is different than I was. He has people who care about him. I made sure he has a home, a good home.''

''Why'd you do that, anyway?''

The question caught him off guard. ''What do you mean?''

''Just that it couldn't have been easy to decide to raise a child on your own.''

''He was my son. There was no decision to make. Once I found out I had a child—''

''Found out?'' she interrupted, eyes widening. ''Didn't you know?''

He didn't want to explain those three years when Josh was lost to him. He had revealed enough to this woman. Yet he couldn't hold it back, either. For too many years, he had carried this anguish alone. Even Gerald didn't know the details.

''Grandfather said Josh came here when he was three,'' Taylor said. ''I just assumed you and your wife were divorced and she decided to give you custody. Are you saying you didn't know you had a son?''

''Exactly,'' Seth muttered. ''That was one little detail she neglected to mention when we divorced.''

An old, nearly forgotten pain began in his chest. And with it came the memories. Montana in late July.

A breeze like the breath from hell. The buzz of a bee among the clover in his Aunt Shirley's yard. The smell of frying onions. And the sight of Josh cowering behind a rusted, broken water pump. If Seth lived to be a hundred he would never forget how his son had run from him.

He looked up at Taylor, daring her to criticize anything he had done for his child. "When Josh was almost three years old, I got a letter from my aunt—yeah, the same aunt who raised me. She said my ex-wife had driven up to the house one day and left a little boy. She claimed he was mine, and since she didn't want him..." He shook his head, remembering the shock and denial he had felt upon reading that letter. "Poor Aunt Shirley. Everyone was always dumping their castoffs on her. First me, then Josh."

Taylor's hand flew to her throat. "Don't," she whispered. "Don't call yourself that—"

"Why not? It's the truth. There wasn't anyone on this Earth who wanted me." Seth clenched his hands into fists at his sides. "But it wasn't going to be that way for Josh. I promised myself it wouldn't."

The muscles worked in Taylor's throat as she swallowed. "What about his mother?"

Hate squeezed his heart. "Last anyone saw of her, she was heading east in a cloud of Montana dust. I hope to God she's dead."

"Seth—"

"She deserves to die," he insisted. "She kept my child from me for three years. Three years in which

God knows what happened to him. He was skin and bones and scared of his own shadow when I got to Montana."

He gave a bitter laugh. "His *mother* didn't want him. Sometimes I wonder whether that word should even apply to her. Once, during a rainstorm, I saw a cat and her kittens caught in some fast water. The mother cat was strong enough to swim against the tide, and she kept going back in the water until she dragged each of her kittens to safety. She kept trying to rescue them, even though they were dead. Funny how that instinct is so strong in animals and so lacking in so many humans."

Closing his eyes, he tried to clear the memory of Josh's mother from his head. "I hate her," he whispered. "I hated her before I knew about Josh. But after that..." His voice trailed away. There were no words to capture his feelings.

"You must have cared for her once. You married her." Taylor's voice seemed to come from a great distance. Caught by his painful memories, Seth had forgotten she was here.

He blinked his eyes and focused on her question. "I'm not sure if I loved Julia," he said at last. "I think she was a convenience. She was pretty and bright. Dark hair, big dark eyes—like Josh's. She made me forget the war. She made me feel important."

"What went wrong?"

"She discovered being married wasn't really much fun, so she found other men to keep her amused."

The simple statement didn't begin to cover the inadequacy Seth had felt when his young wife left him. He couldn't explain that to Taylor. All he could tell her was that Josh's mother had complained. About the place they lived. The car they drove. The money Seth made. He took on two jobs, and she had come back. Once. Twice. Then she betrayed him with a man he had thought was a friend. Seth had called it quits, got a quick divorce in Mexico and left for Alaska. He had never dreamed she was pregnant. When he had received his aunt's letter, he had wondered if Josh was his.

"Then I saw Josh's face," Seth said. "Then I knew he was mine and Julia's child."

"What does Josh know about her?" Taylor whispered.

"Very little."

"You should tell him something."

He looked at her in amazement. "I wouldn't hurt him that way."

"I don't mean you should tell him everything. But he's old enough, smart enough to handle at least part of the truth. Surely he's already asked questions."

"He's asked. I lied and said she was dead."

"And what would happen if she showed up, someday, looking for her son?"

The possibility was like a rocket, exploding into a thousand tiny fragments in Seth's brain. "You don't know," he whispered, staring at Taylor. "You can't imagine how many nightmares I've had about her coming to take him away from me. I'd kill her first," He rubbed a hand over his face, shaking his head. "But it'll never happen. She won't come."

Taylor pressed on, however. "How would Josh feel if he knew you had lied to him about her?"

"He won't know."

"How can you take that chance?" Hands spread wide, Taylor slipped from the stool again. "Seth, I loved my mother. Maybe it's because she was so young when I was born, but we were as much best friends as mother and daughter. I thought we were so close. Do you know how I feel now that I know she kept me from Gerald, from my heritage?"

Her voice broke and tears glimmered in her eyes. "Maybe she hated him, but I deserved to know about him. I deserved to make my own decision about whether I wanted him in my life. I still love her. I'll always love her. But she was wrong to keep this from me. Trust me, if Josh ever finds out the truth, he'll be crushed."

Seth couldn't ignore the entreaty in her voice. But he couldn't accept what she said, either. Because one fear remained. "If he knew Julia was alive, he might try to find her. I can't risk that." The gaze he raised to Taylor was bleak with misery. "Julia uses people, chews them up and spits them out. She would use Josh, hurt him."

More than ever before, Taylor ached for this man. He had lost his childhood. Gone to war too young. Married a woman who betrayed him. Then he had found friends, a home and a child. Was it any wonder he clung so tightly to them all? When everything you have is always being snatched away, you guard your possessions zealously.

She wondered that he could trust anyone. She wanted him to trust her. She wanted to show him love didn't always lead to betrayal.

"I'm sorry," she said, her voice soft. "I'm sorry I made you dredge all this up."

The misery in his gray eyes deepened. "You're like most women. You keep pushing till you find a man's vulnerable spot."

His bitter assessment stung. "That's not why I'm here. I want to help you, help Josh. I don't want what happened to Gerald and my mother to happen to you two."

"But why?" Seth asked. "Less than a month ago, you didn't know us."

"But now I do, and I want to help...."

"That's crazy. Why are we so important to you?"

Cheeks flaming, she lifted her chin. "I think you know why."

"But I don't."

"Because of us," she exclaimed. "Because you and I—"

His sarcastic laugh cut her off. "Oh, now I get it. You think a couple of kisses give you the right to stick your nose in my affairs."

His words hurt. "That's not it...." She drew a ragged breath. "I'm concerned because I care about you. I care a great deal...."

Seth's expression changed, softened. Gently he reached out and framed Taylor's face in his hands. "Don't do this," he said, his voice fierce. "Don't confuse sex with love."

"I'm not confused."

"Yes, you are," he insisted. His hands threaded into her hair, his touch belying his words. "You're not falling in love with me, Taylor. You're smarter than that."

"And maybe I'm smarter than you. Because I am falling in love."

The sound he made was somewhere between a sigh and a groan. It was smothered as he drew Taylor's mouth to his. For her the kiss was a benediction, an affirmation of her feelings. With this kiss she could prove what Seth denied. She could prove her love.

Yet he set her away from him with a force that was almost violent. "You see," he muttered. "This isn't love."

"But it is." She lifted her lips again.

This time, his mouth was brutal against hers. And his hands were everywhere, tunneling through her hair, sliding down her back, around to her breasts. There was nothing of love in his touch.

Infuriated, she struggled to get away. "Stop it, Seth, please, just stop...."

He silenced her with another kiss. Taylor responded despite her anger. The very wildness of his fierce kiss spoke to the part of her that Seth had brought to life.

He didn't stop kissing her until he had backed her against the wall. His body was flush with hers, his hips pressing hard at the juncture of her slightly spread thighs. Her excitement waned. For the first time, the look in Seth's eyes truly frightened her.

She pushed at his chest, but that was like shoving at a brick wall. "Please," she pleaded finally. "Let me go."

But he wasn't through. His superior strength held her so effortlessly. "Does this feel like love?" he muttered. Again he ground his hips into hers. "Does it?"

She thought she would rather die than let him see her cry, but nevertheless, tears blurred her vision. "Why are you doing this?"

"Just answer the question. Does this feel like love?"

Forcing her voice through her throat took every ounce of her strength. "No."

"Then maybe now you understand."

He released her with a suddenness that almost sent her crashing to the floor. Wheeling away from her, his shoulders sagged. "Get out of here."

She couldn't draw enough breath into her lungs to reply.

"Get out," Seth repeated. "Better yet, go home. Go back to your city. It's been hell around here ever since you came."

Taylor found her voice. "You don't mean that."

But when he whirled around, she couldn't deny the anger in his gray eyes. "From the minute you got here nothing's been the same. I don't want you here, Taylor. And you don't want me, either, at least not on the terms I can offer."

"You just want to scare me off," she said, quickly gathering her strength again.

"You looked pretty scared a few minutes ago."

"I'm not frightened now. You're the one who's scared. You're so afraid that if I get too close, you'll want me to stay."

"Spare me the amateur psychology," he said, turning away.

But she grabbed his arm, forced him to look at her again. "The people you want to stay never do, do they, Seth? Not your parents, not Julia, not even Gerald or Josh. Caring about me is just too big a risk, isn't it?"

A muscle twitched in his cheek as he glared at her. "Would you just go?"

She defied him again. "You need me, Seth. I know you need me."

"You're wrong," he muttered. "I don't need you. All I want to do is f—"

She swung her hand up to slap him, cutting off his last hateful, hurtful words. He caught her hand before it connected with his face, however. And they stood that way, locked in a winnerless struggle. Until Taylor ended it. She backed away, feeling as if her heart were going to shatter inside.

The look on her face made Seth want to die. She was like a broken doll. He had only wanted to scare her away. He hadn't meant to hurt her this way.

He stepped forward, but she cringed. That movement sent pain knifing through him.

"Taylor," he whispered. "Taylor, I didn't—"

But his apology was lost. Before the words could form, she was gone.

Several minutes passed as Seth stood, unmoving, while the shed door slammed shut and Taylor's footsteps faded in the distance. He knew he could stay here, not run after her, and this...this *thing* with Taylor might be over for good. She might even hate him. That was what he wanted, wasn't it? He wanted to be done with her once and for all.

I should stay here. Stay here and let it be.

Those words drummed in his head, even as he headed out the door.

Chapter Eight

"...We didn't plan it. I didn't have time to think it through. I think it was just meant to be. I'll remember tonight for the rest of my life. And I know I'll never regret it...."

In exploring the lodge these past few weeks, Taylor had discovered many places that provided quiet solitude. Her grandmother's graveside. The rock near the eagle's nest. And a small, grassy clearing, surrounded by forest, well away from the lodge and its many buildings.

Gerald said he had cleared this area not long after he and Sarah arrived in the valley, thinking they might build a cabin or two here. His plans had changed, yet down through the years he had kept the spot cleared, making sure it was sown with grass and mown periodically. Among lodge guests it was a favorite place for picnics, bird-watching and moments of solitude. Tonight it was empty.

This clearing had been mentioned many times in Holly's diary as a meeting place for her and her lover. Taylor suspected this was where she had been conceived. And now, with Seth's cruel words still echoing in her head, it was the only place she wanted to be.

She didn't cry. Tears had been in her eyes when she ran out of the machine shed, but they were gone by the time she reached the middle of the clearing. She stood, hands clasped tightly together, taking in great, gasping breaths of air. Her face was burning. She felt as raw and sore as someone who had been whipped. But she wouldn't cry. She refused to cry.

Finally, when she had herself under control, she sat down on the grass and hugged her knees to her chest. The peacefulness of the setting began to seep into her bones. Her watch set the time as well past midnight, but the sky, as usual, was still light. The surrounding forest was shadowy, however. Birds called to one another. Leaves danced in a breeze that carried the scents of wood smoke and damp, rich earth.

Seth had been wrong about more than one thing tonight. He had said she didn't know this land well enough to love it. But she did. These past few days, as Josh had taken her from place to place, she had been struck by the contrasts at work here. Stark, snowy mountains soared above the lush vegetation of the rain forest. The modern facades of downtown Juneau sat only miles from the frozen beauty of Mendenhall Glacier. Bears, eagle and moose coexisted with cruise ships and tourist buses.

Taylor knew she could spend a thousand summers here and not tire of all she might discover. Sometimes she couldn't imagine how her mother had brought herself to leave this wild and beautiful land. Only love could have exerted a force strong enough to tear her away. What a pity that love hadn't lasted, had turned out to be such a fraud.

Closing her eyes, Taylor tried to imagine her mother as she might have been twenty-six years ago. She knew from the diary that Holly had vacillated between exhilaration and despair much of the time. Fairly typical for a teenager, but Taylor wasn't seventeen, yet she could now identify with her mother's feelings.

Unlike Holly, however, Taylor had thought herself in love before. What a reasonable experience that seemed in retrospect, a union born of convenience and mutual interests. Everyone, including her mother and Joe, had approved. Yet Taylor had ended the relationship because she was bored. She couldn't imagine being bored with Seth. Yet her grandfather warned her about loving him, and Seth said they weren't meant to be. It was all so confusing, so wrong.

Turning her face up to the cool breeze, she thought again of her mother's long-ago, doomed love affair.

Holly hadn't known that the man, who was ten years older, was married until after they left Alaska. By the time she knew who and what he really was, their love was unraveling. Yet Holly had learned to love again. "How did you survive it, Mother?" Taylor whispered. "How did you make it through?"

Instead of giving her an answer, the wind grew calm. But still Taylor sat, her eyes closed, trying to summon the strength her mother always seemed to have. Surely, here in this place that Holly had loved, Taylor should be able to feel her strength. Here, she was certain she would figure out why Seth had treated her with such cruelty.

When she opened her eyes, Seth stepped from the shelter of the trees.

Taylor stood, thinking she might run away, yet feeling foolish at the thought. He wasn't going to hurt her. He might have frightened her earlier, but she knew instinctively that Seth would never really harm her.

He stopped a foot or so away, his gray eyes regarding her with wariness. His words were simple. "I'm sorry, Taylor."

Because she didn't trust her voice not to break, she nodded, then folded her arms beneath her breasts.

"I didn't mean all of what I said. Some of it I had to say, but I certainly didn't mean to..." He cleared his throat. "I behaved badly. I shouldn't have."

She nodded again, and looked down. Considering all that had passed between them tonight, it hurt too much to face him.

"The thing is," Seth continued, "I think you and I have gotten caught up in something that neither of us understands. There's only one thing I know for sure— you don't love me."

She looked at him then. "Haven't you said that enough for one evening?"

"Taylor." Her name escaped him like a sigh. "I don't want to hurt you, you know."

She managed a laugh. "Then I'd hate to see what you do to people you really want to hurt."

He had the grace to look ashamed. "I just wanted you to see things as they are. I know I went too far, and as I said before, I'm sorry."

Wearily, she dragged a hand through her hair. "You're the one who's not willing to see the truth, Seth. But I don't want to argue with you anymore. Most of all, I don't want to be humiliated by you."

Head held high, she started to walk past him, but he caught her arm. He wasn't rough, as he had been in the shed, but he made her stop. His eyes were silvery slits in his face, his voice was low. "Humiliating you wasn't what I intended."

"Well, that's what you did," she retorted, sliding her arm from his grasp. Because of the slant of the land, she was able to look him straight in the eye. "I was honest with you. Maybe I didn't say what you wanted to hear, but I meant every word. And you threw it all back in my face. You made me feel like a fool."

With a muttered oath, he held his hand out to her, then closed it into a fist. "I'm sorry. I know my apology isn't much, but it's all I have. I'm the one who's a fool. But then, I've been a fool most of my life, and I'm too old to change."

His defeated tone angered her. "You could change if you wanted," she jeered. "But it's safer not to. You just keep telling yourself that all the bad things that happened in your past are going to keep happening. And that's not true."

With her head flung back and fury burning raw in her belly, she stepped closer. She grasped the front of his shirt with both hands. He wasn't going to turn from her now. He was going to listen. "I'm not like anyone else you've ever known, Seth Hardy. I'm not your ex-wife, I'm not any of the people who have hurt you, let you down or screwed up your life. I'm just me. And I care. Right now, even though I'm so hurt and so mad at you that I could scream, I still care."

His expression was one she had never seen before—a mixture of wonder and despair. Not saying a word, he lifted his hands to where she still held tight to his shirt. His fingers folded over hers. And the strength Taylor had asked for earlier flowed through her. The breeze kicked up again, blowing her hair about her face, and it seemed that all the answers she sought lay right before her eyes.

Without pausing to think, she kissed him. Despite all he had said and done earlier, she kissed with love in her heart. He was a man without trust. But she believed. At this moment, she thought she could make him believe with her.

His protest was expected. He drew away, muttering, "We can't do this...."

She silenced him with another kiss. With tender, questing lips, she kissed his mouth, his chin, even the pulse that beat an erratic rhythm at his throat.

He groaned another protest, but the hands that gripped hers loosened. His arms slipped round her, and soon he was kissing her back. Like a man too long without nourishment, his mouth was ravenous on hers. They kissed for so long, with such abject hunger, that he didn't bother to protest when she drew him down on the soft, damp carpet of grass.

He eased her back till she lay half beneath him on the ground, his body shielding hers from the wind. Taylor thought later that it must have been cold. But she didn't notice. All she knew was the beauty of Seth's kiss.

He took such care in kissing her. Slowly, reverently, his mouth moved over hers. His fingers were warm against her throat as he lifted her face to his. The kiss went on forever, yet not long enough.

When he broke away, she murmured a protest. But he silenced her with a gentle touch of his fingers to her lips. His eyes were dark with concern. "Are you sure this is what you want?"

How like him to ask. How perfectly unexpected, just like he is.

Taylor lifted her hand to his square, determined jaw. The stubble of his beard was rough to her touch. But the skin beneath it was soft. Tough yet tender—that was the sum of this man. She smiled up at him. "I've never been surer of anything in my life."

He smiled back. Then he kissed her again, while his steady, practiced fingers drifted down, opening the buttons of her blouse and releasing her bra's front closure. His thumb barely skimmed the hardening peaks of her breasts. Once. Twice. First one, then the other. Then it was his mouth that moved with damp, warm insistence against the sensitive nub of flesh. He eased the zipper of her jeans downward. She helped him shove them down and out of the way, and his touch was on her, in her.

A thrumming, liquid spiral began in the delta between her thighs. Head back, spine arching, she felt the wildness take hold inside of her. The feeling mingled with the smell of the earth beneath them, with the deep blue of the night sky that stretched overhead. She felt in tune with the world around them, but most dramatically, with herself. Her heart pumped a furious cadence. She could hear herself breathing, could hear the moans that built in her throat and escaped.

Those sounds were almost Seth's undoing.

He wanted with all his heart to take this slow, to savor the texture and taste of her. He wanted to make it right, to make it good. But the weeks of wanting, of pent-up frustrations and agonized soul-searching played havoc with his control.

Maybe it was the same for Taylor. For soon her hands were on him, loosening his jeans, releasing the hot, heavy length of him to her touch. There was no time, no thought for niceties or hesitations. Just a movement of clothing, an adjustment of bodies, and he thrust into her.

She met him with a strength he didn't expect. With silken, velvet power, she accepted him, moved with him.

They coupled with something akin to desperation. With words that were urgent and low. With cries that rose from deep in his throat, cries she seemed to complete for him. Their harmony startled him. Then he didn't think, couldn't think of anything but the release that emptied down him, through him, into her.

For several moments afterward, he didn't move. He knew his weight was too heavy on Taylor. Yet he didn't want to move away, either. When this moment was over, he would have to face the consequences of what they had done, what *he* had done. Finally, knowing he couldn't avoid the inevitable, he slipped to her side.

The look of her almost took his breath. Her skin was pale in the dim light, marked here and there with rosy color, evidence of their fierce loving. Her eyes were somnolent, content, the lazy eyes of a satisfied woman. Yet she couldn't be satisfied. He had been too fast, too harsh.

"I'm sorry..." he began.

But she placed a hand over his mouth. "Stop it. I don't want to hear your regrets. You're not going to ruin this with regrets."

Gently he drew her hand away. "I ruined it with my impatience."

"I don't feel ruined."

Sighing her name, he drew her back into his arms. "I can't believe I let this happen this way."

"It was my decision, remember?"

"But I should have—"

Her bright trill of laughter cut off his final protest. "If you keep talking about what went wrong, I'm going to stop thinking it was the highlight of my life."

He managed a smile before he fell silent. With wonder, he pressed his face to her neck. Her skin was soft. Her fragrance was the same as the wind and the trees. She felt fragile in his arms, very slight, easily hurt. Yet he could remember the strength of her body beneath his own. He would never forget her fine, young strength.

Dear God, what was he doing here with her?

The hows and wheres and whens of it didn't really matter. It just should never have happened at all. All the arguments he had used before still applied. And yet he had gone ahead with this. Now that he knew this last, final sweetness she had to offer, how was he going to bear it when she left?

Taylor shivered in his arms. He drew away. "You're freezing. We should go in."

"No. If we go in, this will be over. And I'm not ready to let you go. Not until you promise me you'll stop regretting this."

She read him so well. Too well. "Taylor, this was a crazy thing to do. It's exactly what I didn't want to happen. Sex blurs a person's judgment."

"Maybe I want to be blurred."

"You don't understand. You're too young—"

"I'm not some inexperienced schoolgirl, Seth. Did I act like a schoolgirl a few minutes ago?"

"No, but—"

Her eyes flashed. "Stop looking for ways to save me from myself. You're the only person who has ever tried to save me that way. You can't play the tyrant with me."

That stung. "I'm not being a tyrant. I just want to protect—"

"You can't protect me," she said. "I don't want you to protect me. I know what I'm doing. I know what I want." Once more she lifted her lips to his. Her words were soft against his mouth. "Please, Seth, just let your doubts go, let us *be* for a while. Who knows, maybe I'll change your mind about a lot of things."

He was weary of fighting her, weary of resisting when what he wanted most was to seek the haven she offered in her embrace. So he kissed her. And held her. Beneath the summer sky, he felt excitement stir him again.

With rapidly growing ardor he pressed his mouth down her body. This time, he wasted long delicious moments on the salty, silky taste of her. He lingered over her small, rounded breasts. Her nipples, like tiny coral flowers, budded against his tongue, while Taylor's fingers splayed through his hair, holding him to her. Her whispered encouragement sent him downward. Here, she was sleek and slender, her belly taut, the skin firm and smooth. But he moved on, his mouth open, savoring, till he tasted himself in the hot, secret cleft between her thighs.

His tongue had only begun its playful dance when Taylor began to tremble. Pleasure spun through her. Like the colors twirled together for Monet's greatest masterpiece, the effect was delicate, almost difficult to grasp. Yet she clung to the sensation, let it spin her around. And she wanted more.

With a touch made insistent by desire, she soon pressed Seth back to the ground. And it was her turn to explore. The crisp, dark hair on his chest. The crescent-shaped scar just above his right leg. The ticklish spot low on his side. She discovered them all, exploited them all in making love to him.

He sighed when her questing, eager fingers closed over his sex. Groaned when she slipped her body over his. Was silent when she fitted their bodies together.

He came off the ground then, so that they faced one another, torso to torso. His hands on her hips. Hers on his shoulders. And they moved together. To a shattering, intense completion.

Afterward, she wanted to sleep. She wanted to find a bed and crawl under the covers with Seth. She could only imagine what kind of heaven that would be. With his strong warm body curled around hers, his heart beating just inches away.

But Josh was in Seth's cabin. Her grandfather was in hers. And though both of them would have to know sooner or later that Taylor and Seth were involved, this wasn't the time.

She induced Seth to stay in the clearing for as long as she could. But even passion couldn't combat the damp, chilly air forever. All too soon, Taylor stood on the cabin porch, watching him make his way through the trees.

She slept only a few hours and woke to the sound of rain on the tin roof. She turned on her side, snuggling into her quilt. The hot, soapy shower she had taken before going to bed hadn't erased the pleasant ache she felt in her bones. Was Seth feeling that, too? She smiled at the thought.

But she knew he was feeling other emotions, as well. Last night's loving wouldn't have eased Seth's doubts. She frowned, remembering the way he had told her to leave, to go home. When he had followed her to the clearing, he hadn't apologized for saying that. He had been sorry for the rough way he had treated her, but he hadn't taken back all that he had said.

In the final estimation, they had resolved nothing.

She knew that should make her sad. But she wasn't.

She didn't know anyone who could truly be sad after last night. She felt sated. She felt whole. And she wanted to be with Seth.

After pulling on jeans and a sweater, she found her grandfather was already gone. So she ran through the rain to the lodge, eager to see if Seth waited there, yet oddly nervous, too. It was one thing to face your lover alone on the morning after. It was another to know so many others would be looking on.

He sat with Gerald and Josh, at a corner table near the dining room window. She was pleased to see father and son together. Josh didn't look cheerful, but surely his presence at the table meant something. Maybe part of what she had said last night had made an impact on Seth.

She continued to hesitate in the doorway, absurdly shy about crossing the room to Seth's table. Then he looked up, and their gazes met. Taylor thought she would carry the look he gave her to the grave. A warm look. Gently knowing. Full of tenderness and a certain awe. The room was half-full, but she forgot anyone else was there. Seth must have, too, because he got out of his chair and came toward her.

"Good morning," she managed, though she could feel her lips trembling as she tried to smile.

His gray eyes, which could be as cold as steel, were soft. "I thought you would sleep in."

"I considered it."

Inane words. Unimportant except for the fact that they said them to one another. No reason to stand grinning at each other. Yet they did.

One of the guests mumbled something in passing, and the spell was shattered, reminding them of where they were. Seth took a step backward. Taylor looked around, noticing the interested glances being sent in their direction, especially from the two males who still sat in the corner.

Seth took her arm, and his voice roughened. "Come on, we might as well face the music."

At the table, Gerald treated them both to a long, quizzical look, but said nothing more than good morning. Josh was sprawled back in his seat, his brown eyes narrowed, but he didn't say a word, either; he just nodded at her greeting.

The buoyancy she had felt only minutes ago was smothered by the tension at the table. She sat, toying with the empty mug at her place, thinking this would be much better if someone would speak. If someone would say something, Josh might stop tapping his fork against the edge of his plate. And Seth might stop casting Gerald these guilty, sideways glances. And she would stop feeling as if she were going to jump right out of her chair.

"Glory be, what gloomy Guses you all are."

At the sound of Millie's cheerful voice, Taylor sent her empty coffee mug clattering sideways across the table. Seth caught it before it crashed to the floor. Josh sat forward. Gerald frowned.

"You startled me," Taylor said to Millie.

"Didn't mean to." With apparent unconcern, the woman poured coffee from an insulated pot into Taylor's mug. "What's everyone looking so down at the mouth about?"

The collective shrug started with Josh and worked its way around the table to Taylor, who said, "I guess it's the rain."

Millie chuckled. "If we all got this down every time it rained around here, we'd be in trouble for sure." She wiped her hands on her pink-striped apron, pulled a chair from an adjoining table and sat down. "Okay, now, what's the real problem?" Her twinkling gaze darted from one to the other before settling on Josh. "What's wrong with you?"

The teenager made a face. "Do you have to ask? Dad grounded me for a week." Father and son shared a long, measured glance.

Millie tsk-tsked. "Seems to me you might have gotten worse, what with flying off without a radio and scaring us all to death like you did."

Josh settled once again into his gloomy sprawl. "It's just that I wanted to fly Taylor over to the logging camp and show her around."

Taylor smiled at him in reassurance. "We've got the rest of the summer to see the camp. Surely you can stay out of trouble and ungrounded for that long."

"The rest of the summer?" Gerald asked, straightening his shoulders. "I thought you would be going home in about two weeks."

"I changed my mind." Taylor felt, rather than saw, Seth's intense regard, but she looked at Gerald. "Think you can put up with me a while longer?"

His answer was a beam of delight, making her happier than ever that she had made this decision. She had begun to think about changing her plans just after she realized the seriousness of Gerald's condition. She didn't want to leave him now. She had other reasons for staying, of course, but it was Gerald she had been thinking of when she wrote and asked Joe to take care of her apartment and other details.

But Gerald's pleased smile quickly disappeared. "I don't want you to feel you have to stay, Taylor. I know you miss your father, your friends. You have a career to think of."

"There's nothing pressing right now. And I can work wherever I am. Just give me pencils and paint."

He seemed ready to protest again, but Millie shushed him. "Goodness, Gerald, you know you want her to stay. Stop making a fuss."

He acquiesced, his smile reappearing. "I'm glad you're staying. I want that eagle for my mantel, you know."

"I wouldn't dare forget."

While Millie and Josh expressed their pleasure over her decision to stay, Taylor finally looked at Seth. His expression was unreadable. He disappointed her, although she wasn't sure what she had expected. Uncontested happiness would have been nice. She would have settled for an encouraging smile. Earlier, when he had come all the way across the room to meet her at the door, she had thought...well, it didn't matter what she had thought. She didn't know how to predict Seth's actions. She knew better than to try.

While she sat, filling with an unreasonable but still palpable hurt, he pushed his chair back and stood. She kept smiling, nodding at some plan Josh was hatching for another fishing expedition. Even though she was aware of every move Seth made, the touch of his hand on her shoulder startled her nonetheless.

She tipped her head back to look at him. "Yes?"

"I'm glad you're staying," was all he said. His hand lingered on her shoulder a moment more, too long for the gesture to be construed as casual or meaningless. Then he turned and walked away without a backward glance.

"Well, well..." Millie's soft exclamation brought Taylor back down to earth.

They were all looking at her—Millie, Gerald and Josh. She did her best to seem blithely unaware of any undercurrents, to behave as if Seth's behavior was completely normal.

But she failed.

"Excuse me," she murmured and pushed back her chair. Outside, Seth was crossing the lodge clearing, heading for the river. From the porch Taylor called his name. He stopped, and she went flying down the path. The rain quickly soaked her thin cotton sweater, but she didn't care.

She slid to a stop in front of him. "You can't do that, you know."

"Do what?"

"Do something so completely unexpected and then just walk away."

His smile just curved the corners of his mouth. "I didn't want to shock the group in there too much in one morning."

"Oh, but why ever not?" she asked, and before he could divine her intent, she raised on tiptoe and pressed a hard, possessive kiss on his mouth.

He finally held her away, darting glances from right to left, as if he was afraid they would be caught.

Wiping the rain from her cheeks, Taylor laughed up at him. "Don't worry. Despite your activities of the morning, I think your reputation as a hard ass is still pretty much intact." Then she walked away, a saucy, self-satisfied bounce in her steps.

Seth remained where he was, wondering where in the hell he had misplaced his common sense.

Last night had been bad enough. Not that he would trade last night, not for anything. But this morning, when Taylor walked in, he had felt this…this *joy.* He could remember few times in his life when he had known that emotion. It took him by surprise, made him cross the dining room like some ardent young suitor. Then he had to complicate matters more by telling her, in front of everyone, that he was glad she was staying.

But he was glad. He should be praying for her to leave, to get it over with. Yet he couldn't. He wanted her here. He hated himself for wanting her so much, but he did.

Chapter Nine

"... Nothing can go wrong now. How could anything bad happen when I feel so good? Somehow, I have to make Dad understand...."

The wind that blew off the glaciers was frigid. And exhilarating, Taylor thought, as she drew her insulated parka tighter about her. When Seth had suggested they take a boat up to the face of a tidewater glacier, she hadn't known what to expect. She certainly hadn't planned on the giant wall of ice their rather insignificant-feeling tour boat was fast approaching. Even at two to three miles out, the glacier snout, as she had learned the face was called, loomed over their boat.

"I didn't think it would be so big," she murmured.

Seth and Josh, who were standing on either side of her on the boat deck, laughed.

"I told you it was incredible," Josh said, his teeth chattering. "And cold."

Taylor linked her arm through his. "This is nothing compared to the wind off Lake Michigan in February."

No sooner had she spoken than a loud boom rent the air.

"Look there," Seth shouted, pointing to where massive slabs of ice fell from the glacier's snout and into the cold waters of Glacier Bay. Upon impact, water and spray shot hundreds of feet into the air. Waves swelled outward, rocking the boat so hard that Seth took Taylor's other arm to hold her steady. "Now that's something you can't see on Lake Michigan."

Indeed it was. Another boom sounded, like the firing of dozens of cannons. Once more, ice, perhaps nine or ten stories high, broke away and crashed into the water. It was nature at its most primitive, and it took Taylor's breath away.

The tourists clustered on the boat deck echoed her awe. Cameras whirred and clicked as they tried to capture the spectacle on tape or film. Taylor had brought her camera, but she didn't bother with it. Nothing could match the reality of standing here between Seth and Josh and experiencing the sight first-hand.

Seth bent close to her ear. "The ice fall is called calving. You hear the boom, you see the ice calve away from the snout, then the icebergs float away."

For miles, they had been passing large and small icebergs, some with fat harbor seals enjoying a ride through the bay. Farther back, they had witnessed the magnificent jump and dive of a humpback whale. To Taylor's enchanted eyes, this was yet another Alaska, a land of fjords, islands and inlets. Another Alaska, in contrast to the mountains and forests surrounding the lodge.

Yesterday Gerald had told her the word *Alaska* meant "great lands" in the Aleut Indian language. Taylor thought it appropriate. This was a great land. And the more she saw, the more she *experienced* Alaska, the more at home she felt.

Their boat cut across the water in front of the glacier. Ice continued to fall in spectacular fashion. Taylor thought she could watch for hours.

But Josh nodded toward the boat's glass-encased central cabin. "I'm going in for some hot chocolate. Want to come?"

Taylor and Seth waved him inside. After he was gone, she murmured, "I'm glad he wanted to come with us today."

Seth agreed. "I was surprised."

"You shouldn't be," Taylor said, smiling as she nestled closer to Seth's side.

Since the incident with the broken radio, Josh hadn't pulled any more stunts to anger Seth. It helped that in the past couple of weeks Seth seemed to be reaching out to him, mellowing a bit, not acting as if Josh's normal growing pangs were such a threat. She thought Seth's new attitude was due in part to her influence. She believed Josh had benefited from her objectivity, also.

On one of their many recent walks last week, she had asked Josh to be patient with Seth. She even told him some of what she knew of his father's childhood. Seth might be angry if he knew, but she thought it was important for Josh to understand the background that had shaped his father.

Josh had responded to the information with thoughtful questions. "Why can't Dad tell me this kind of stuff himself?"

"Some people have a hard time talking about themselves, especially about anything painful."

With a resigned sigh, Josh shoved his hands into his jeans pockets. A frown wrinkled his brow. "Dad never talks to me. When Gerald came home from the hospital this spring, I wanted to know the truth about what was happening with him. Dad couldn't tell me, though. He just got that look on his face...you know, the 'stone' look. It was Gerald who told me the truth. Gerald always does." He paused, his dark brown eyes reflecting his sorrow. "It was real tough, hearing how sick Gerald is, but I'm glad I know. I'm prepared, I think."

His thoughtful, grown-up attitude about a painful matter impressed Taylor. Yet she tried to explain Seth's reticence. "I'm sure your father didn't want to hurt you with the truth. He knows how much you care for my grandfather. The same as he cares."

"That's what Gerald said. He's always defending Dad, telling me what a good person he is and how he means well, reminding me that I could have worse fathers."

Taylor longed to tell the boy exactly what Seth had saved him from, but that was one confidence she knew she could never break. "I think your father would do anything for you" was all she allowed herself to say.

"I know that," Josh replied in the tone teenagers use when adults get too serious. But his expression quickly sobered, too. "Dad and I used to be close, you know. We did stuff together. But now it's easier to talk to Gerald, or to you. Dad just doesn't seem to understand what I want. He doesn't take me seriously, either."

"Don't push him so hard. I've found out your father just resists if you try to push."

Josh stopped in the middle of the path, wheeling round to face her. "You and Dad spend a lot of time together these days. What's the deal, anyway?"

She took her time answering, because she was certain Josh already knew the answer. He had known something was up since the night he had surprised her and Seth in his cabin. He had tried monopolizing her time for a while. During that time together, while he took her sightseeing and fishing, his crush had diminished, and the friendship they now enjoyed had emerged. Even Seth believed his son was over his puppy love.

But that didn't mean Josh was ready to see his father involved with anyone. Taylor suspected whatever women had been in Seth's life for the past few years had been kept quite apart from the lodge. How would Josh really feel about her and his father?

When she continued to hesitate before answering him, he said, "I know there's something going on with you and Dad, so don't bother denying it."

"I'm not." She watched his reaction closely. "What do you think?"

He shrugged. "It's okay with me. I mean, I don't remember my mother or anything and, well...I think Dad needs someone like you."

"Gee, thanks," Taylor retorted dryly. "That's quite an endorsement."

Laughing, Josh leaned his shoulder against hers and gave her a playful push. "It's true. You've mellowed him out."

"I'm glad you appreciate my efforts."

"I do. Only, you guys kind of surprised me by getting together. At first you both acted as if you couldn't stand each other."

She grinned, backing away from him along the path. "It happens that way sometimes."

The teenager rolled his eyes and fell in step beside her again. Several minutes of companionable silence passed before he asked quietly, "So, are you really going to be staying or what?"

Taylor made a vague answer that was really no answer at all. Not because she didn't want to tell Josh. But because she didn't know.

And as she stood beside Seth on the boat deck, Josh's question still had no answer. Was she staying? For Gerald's sake, yes. Until he... It was difficult to think of Gerald faltering. He seemed so well these days. And in truth, she was staying for herself, too. Staying and waiting for Seth to tell her he didn't want her to leave. Would he ever do that? She had no idea.

She glanced up at him now. The hood of his parka had slipped back, and the wind stirred his dark hair. His face was ruddy from the cold, his gray eyes filled with awe as he continued to watch the glaciers calve.

In past weeks, they had shared other days such as this. Days of companionship and discovery. They had hiked with guests or alone. Worked side by side pacifying guests when the generator that supplied the lodge's power failed. They had fished, flown over the mountains and visited a Tlingit Indian totem village. Alaska continued to work its magic on her heart. As did Seth. The two of them—the man and this ceaselessly beautiful land—were bound together for her. She loved them both.

But did Seth love her?

Not since the morning when he had said he was glad she was staying had either of them mentioned what might come next. There was no talk of a future, no talk of love or commitment. Each day just unwound into the next. She had told Seth she cared. She was trying to win his trust. The next step was his.

She wasn't sure when she had become so impatient. She had never jumped so quickly into an intimate relationship with a man. Granted, the list of men in her life was very short. But she had moved faster with Seth than she would have ever thought possible. She knew it could be right with him. She dreamed of sharing his life, having his child. She wanted their future to begin right now, immediately. Perhaps her mother's death and Gerald's illness had made her realize how mortal they all were. For whatever the reason, Taylor didn't want to waste one single day.

But as she had told Josh, she knew better than to push Seth for answers. Maybe there were no answers. Maybe he was content just to drift as they were doing now.

That's not good enough, Taylor thought, looking up at him again. She wanted the kind of caring and sharing her mother and Joe had known, the everlasting love Gerald had for his Sarah. Nothing less would do.

Her pensive thoughts cast a shadow on the day. The glaciers lost their allure. Even a delicious dinner at the rambling Glacier Bay Country Inn, a spot renowned for their gourmet dishes, wasn't the event she had been anticipating.

Seth sensed Taylor's unease. On the flight back to the lodge, she fell asleep, and her air of sadness lingered even then. He kept shooting glances her way, wondering what was wrong, what he could have done.

Two months ago, he would never have imagined being in this position, with a woman's feelings to worry about. But never in a million years would he have counted on Taylor coming into his life. With her bold way of standing up to him. With her bright, uninhibited laughter. With her unique balance of enthusiasm and maturity.

She made him feel young again. Hell, she made him act young. The blood rushed to Seth's face as he considered his besotted, sexual obsession with this woman. The lodge, its many guests and the demands on his time left them little privacy. But they had made do when the time and place presented itself. Seth discovered he could forget most of his responsibilities when Taylor gave him a certain, slow, sexy smile. She said she liked the challenge of their adventurous pursuit of privacy.

So they had *challenged* each other in the early morning hours near the eagle's nest.

And in his bed in the middle of the day, where they had to smother their laughter when a fisherman came knocking on the door at a most unfortunate moment.

And just last evening in the machine shed, when the fear of discovery hadn't kept them from exploring the sensual possibilities of the long worktable. Seth wasn't sure he could ever look at that table in quite the same way again.

He often had a hard time meeting Gerald's gaze. His old friend had said only one thing with regards to Seth's relationship with Taylor, "Don't hurt her."

Seth didn't want to hurt Taylor. Yet he couldn't make her any promises and he couldn't extract promises from her. She had said she would change his mind about a lot of things. Yes, she had changed him. But he still knew that promises seldom lasted.

In the clearing on the night they had first made love, Taylor had asked Seth to set his doubts aside. The only way he could manage that was to live minute to minute, day to day. She wasn't the kind of woman one played fast and loose with, but he did everything he could not to think past this day or the next. If he didn't plan a future with Taylor, the reality of one without her might not hurt so much.

She had told him she cared. But he knew it wouldn't last. It had never lasted.

A tap on Seth's shoulder brought him out of his musings. He looked round at Josh, who was in the seat behind Taylor's. Over the noise of engine and wind, Josh called, "Are you going to fly right past the lodge or what?"

Seth muttered a curse as he realized the lodge and the river were being left behind. It wasn't like him to become so distracted while in the air. He might have collided with someone. This might be wilderness, but there were plenty of crafts crowding the airways. One couldn't be too careful, especially on a night like this, when fog was beginning to settle in.

After they landed, Josh gave him a hard time about overshooting the lodge. Taylor joined in, too, her earlier melancholy mood gone. Seth responded in kind, and they made a raucous group as they crowded up the path to the lodge. Gerald, on the porch with a group of guests, demanded to know what the noise was about. And Millie appeared, wiping her hands on her ever-present apron and offering pie and coffee in the dining room. There, the high spirits continued. Guests rambled in and out, but in the end, it was just the five of them—Gerald and Taylor, Millie, Josh and himself.

The family, Seth thought. *My family.*

He didn't dwell on the implications of mentally adding Taylor to this circle. He just sat back, content for once to savor the moment. He belonged here. This was the only place he had ever belonged in his life.

Later, after kissing Taylor good-night, he whistled as he walked through the trees to his cabin. The tune was an old one that he couldn't quite place. On the porch he paused, trying to recall the song title and re-alizing he hadn't whistled in a long, long time. Maybe not since his eighteenth summer when he had thought himself in love.

He could remember whistling then. Driving home late at night from his girl's house in the rattletrap pickup he had salvaged from the junkyard, with the Montana sky overhead and a warm glow down inside him. He had thought anything was possible then.

A few months later, when her love proved false, he knew better.

The bitter memory of past failures silenced his whistle. Why was it, he wondered, that his happiness could never survive his memories? He ached for the boy he had been, who believed in dreams, and for the man he was now, who knew dreams were lies.

Even a dream as sweet as Taylor's kiss.

Stepping back from the drawing she had propped on an easel on Seth's porch, Taylor cocked her head to the side. The work intrigued her. It was her own. She knew every line, every shading. Yet this drawing of her grandfather's eagle was unlike anything she had ever done.

Since her late teens, it had been the city that intrigued her creative self. The bustling crowds, the dramatic architecture, the high levels of energy. Her media of choice were charcoal and graphite, with pastels shaded in for emphasis and drama. She had tried working in oils, but paints never gave her the feeling of freedom she had when holding a pen or pencil in her hand. Teachers and others she respected had often praised the sense of movement in her work. It was exactly that quality she had hoped to convey in this eagle.

She had succeeded beyond her wildest dreams.

Poised over his nest, talons extended, wings lifted, her eagle was intended to represent untamed power and raw beauty. That impression was more important to Taylor than an accurate depiction of each feather or curve of the creature's physical self. Through this eagle she wanted to express her awe, her respect and her love of this incredible land. Her mother's first home. Her grandfather's pride. Her heritage.

The eagle wasn't her only triumph. She had begun a half dozen other drawings, of the mountains and the river, of glaciers calving and bear cubs romping through a meadow. Each attempt held a verve, an excitement that made all her previous work pale in comparison.

If she needed any proof of how this summer had changed her, she had only to look to her work. She would never be the same. She stared at the drawing a long time, wondering where these changes would take her. Both professionally and personally. She knew where she wanted to go. But her plans would take the cooperation of others.

She had zipped the drawing into one of the protective pockets of her portfolio when Seth called to her from the path. "I see you're hiding from me again."

She grinned. There was nothing she wanted more than to share this piece of work with Seth. But she thought her grandfather should be the first to appreciate his eagle. And she wanted the moment to be right. "You'll see it when everyone else does."

"I hope it's soon," Seth complained, coming up the stairs. "Gerald may be reduced to stealing your portfolio."

"He wouldn't stoop so low."

"No, but I would." He bent to kiss her, a mischievous grin on his face. "I'm a tyrant, remember?"

Her fingers closed on the lapels of his jacket, holding him close. She dropped her voice. "I have ways of dealing with men who try to dominate me."

He chuckled. "I can handle it. In fact, I would probably enjoy it."

Taylor's laughter was caught by his kiss. She loved him like this—teasing and playful. This was a side he revealed all too infrequently. In the weeks since their trip to the glacier, they'd had so little time alone. She had begun to think he was avoiding her. Yet here he was, laughing with her, kissing her with a thoroughness that made her head spin.

Seth had so many facets, and he could change so quickly. Like this land, like the evolving nature of her work, he intrigued her, excited her.

Pulling back, she murmured, "I guess it's too much to hope that Josh is away for the rest of the afternoon."

His eyes widened in pretended shock. "Why, Miss Cantrell, are you issuing an invitation?"

"There have been people around us ever since that night we came back from the glacier."

"Can I help it if I run a successful business?"

"I keep praying for some cancellations."

"Shame on you." Belying his words, his mouth lowered to hers once again.

Taylor's arms slipped around his neck. *It shouldn't take my breath away. It shouldn't always make me tremble. God, the things he can do to me with just his kiss. . . .*

The kiss deepened until Josh's chiding voice drew them apart. "Break it up, you two. It's the middle of the day."

Seth broke away with a muttered curse. "Son, you're going to have to learn to use a bit more tact."

"Sorry," Josh replied. "But you never taught me the proper way to break up a kiss."

"The proper way is not to break it up at all."

The boy bounded up the stairs, tossed a stack of mail onto one rocking chair and sat in the other. He folded his arms and grinned at them. "Don't mind me. I'll just sit here and take notes."

Groaning, Taylor stepped away from Seth and swatted Josh across the knees. She liked the new ease with which Josh dealt with her and Seth, but she would have enjoyed an hour or two without his company. "Your son really knows how to spoil a mood," she told Seth.

"I thought you might want your mail," Josh said huffily.

"This is all mine?" Grinning in delight, Taylor snatched up the assortment of envelopes and sat down to sift through them.

Seth knew it was absurd to resent an innocent stack of mail, but he did. In those envelopes were Taylor's other life, the people and places who were quite apart from the lodge. Far away from him.

Leaning on the porch railing, he watched her sort the mail into two stacks and felt his spirits sag. Just a few minutes ago, he had felt on top of the world. Not for any reason other than that Taylor had looked up at him and smiled. But here was reality, as clear as the pleasure with which Taylor began reading her letters from family and friends.

In the middle of the first letter, she sat up, her expression registering first joy, then dismay.

Seth was instantly on the alert. "What's wrong?"

She glanced at him, her smile tremulous. "It's the gallery owner who wanted me to do an exhibition this winter. He's had some changes in plans, and he wants to move the show up."

Seth's heart begin to thud in a painful rhythm.

"That's good news, isn't it?" Josh asked. "You told me a one-woman show was kind of a big deal."

Scanning the letter again, Taylor corrected him absently, "It's a one-*person* show, Josh. The other way is sexist."

"Well, whatever, it's pretty good, isn't it?"

"Yeah."

"So how come you're not excited?"

She took a deep breath. "I'd have to go back at the end of August to get ready."

Josh glanced at Seth, his eyes widening. Seth gripped the porch railing even harder. *The end of August. Only three and a half weeks away.*

"Do you have to go?" Josh asked finally, his tone somber.

Taylor pushed a hand through her hair and continued to frown down at the letter. "I need to look at the gallery space again, and go through all my work with the owner. There are things that will have to be framed. It's not something I can do long-distance. And besides..." She darted a glance toward the portfolio that leaned against the wall of the cabin.

Finally she looked back at Seth. "None of my old work is good enough."

He forced himself to speak. He was aching, but he made himself reassure her, "That's crazy, Taylor. You're good, you know you're good or this guy wouldn't be having an exhibition of your work. You should be very excited."

"But everything's changed," she protested. "The new pieces I'm working on...the eagle..." Again she glanced toward the portfolio. "It's all so different. I'm not even the same person who did those other drawings."

Seth didn't believe her. Weeks ago, when she had first mentioned this show to him, she had been filled with excitement. The exhibition was her big chance, a stepping-stone to professional success. He didn't believe she had changed so much that this opportunity wasn't still very important. He knew how she cared about her work. Though he hadn't seen the eagle she had drawn for Gerald, he had seen her absorption in the creative process. These changes she had mentioned couldn't have altered her ambitions. Ambitions that would take her away.

She stood now, clutching her letters, looking distracted. "I want you both to come to Gerald's cabin before dinner tonight."

"How come?" Josh asked.

She picked up her portfolio. "It's time for an unveiling."

Though she kissed Seth and smiled at him before she left, a heavy dread settled in his gut. The porch seemed empty when she was gone.

"I don't want her to leave."

Josh's quiet words made Seth turn. His son's dark eyes were a perfect reflection of the misery Seth was feeling. But he couldn't admit to those feelings. The best protection had always been pretending he didn't care. So he made himself shrug. "Taylor's real life isn't here."

"She'll come back," Josh said, but there was uncertainty rather than confidence in his tone.

Regret roughened Seth's voice. "Don't count on it."

"But she loves it here. She's told me she does."

"It's been a vacation, a chance to get to know Gerald—"

"But what about us?" There was genuine pain in Josh's expression now. "I thought she cared about us."

Seth wanted to spare Josh the agony he was about to go through, but he knew he couldn't. When Taylor left and didn't return, as he knew would happen, his son would be hurt. Gently he tried to explain, "You have to remember that Taylor spent a lifetime back in Chicago. She has a family—''

''Gerald's her family.''

''Son, she has a father, too—the man who adopted her and raised her as his own. His family is her family. She has friends, and she has her work.''

''But she can work anywhere.''

Seth sighed. ''Do you really believe that, son? She has to go home, to do this exhibition. It's what she wants.''

''But she could come back,'' Josh said stubbornly.

Seth said nothing.

With a suddenness that sent the rocker where he was seated crashing against the cabin wall, Josh stood. He faced Seth with a defiant tilt to his chin. ''Don't you want her to stay?''

Seth tried to lie, tried to say he didn't care, but for once in his life he couldn't pretend. ''Yeah,'' he muttered, looking away. ''I want her to stay.''

''Then ask her.''

He shook his head.

''But why?'' Josh asked. ''She'd stay if you asked, maybe if you married her.''

The suggestion startled Seth. ''I'm not marrying anyone.''

''But you and Taylor...you...'' Josh stumbled and fumbled over his words. He flushed when he found the ones he sought. ''I mean, you love her, don't you?''

The question ran like cold fire through Seth. It burned and stung. He didn't believe in love. Love didn't exist. What he felt for Taylor wasn't, couldn't be love. Harshly he said, "Love doesn't have anything to do with me and Taylor."

Josh sucked in his breath, the red in his cheeks deepening. "So what is she to you? Something like that woman who runs the restaurant in Juneau?"

Shocked into silence, Seth stared at his son.

The boy laughed. Coldly. A sound Seth recognized as one of his own. "I guess you didn't think I knew about her, did you?" Josh asked, his mouth twisting bitterly. "One of the pilots told me last summer. You had flown in to Juneau, and I asked what for. He said you were going to 'get some.' I must have had a stupid look on my face, 'cause the guy just laughed and told me you had a good thing going with a redhead on Seward Street."

Seth was angry. Angry with the thoughtless jerk who had told a young boy about his relationship with Bobbie Jo. Angry with himself for forgetting how people could talk.

"I went into her restaurant last year," Josh said. "She was nice, not like...well, not like I expected. But she's not like Taylor, either." Seth hadn't seen Josh cry since he was a little boy, but now his eyes were suspiciously bright. And his hands doubled into fists at his sides. "You can't treat Taylor like her, Dad."

"It isn't like that, son. I promise you it isn't."

"Then how is it?"

"It's just different...special."

Josh looked unconvinced. "Special how, Dad? The special like you told me it should be before I had sex with anyone? Or special like good, like really go—"

"Stop it," Seth cut in, angry now. "You're not going to talk this way to me. My relationship with Taylor is private."

"But I want her to stay," Josh said. "She's the best thing that's ever happened around here. If it's so *special* with Taylor, why can't you ask her to stay?"

Seth didn't know how to explain to his son that asking for love and commitment gave people weapons with which to hurt you. He had hoped against hope that this was a caveat Josh might not have to live with. He now understood the duplicity in teaching a child to live as one said, not as one did. Yet that didn't change what was going to happen with Taylor.

"I can't ask her," he said. He made his voice firm. "I don't want to ask her to stay."

Josh took a step backward. His eyes, those dark, trusting eyes of his, narrowed. And for the first time in years, he reminded Seth of Julia. The resemblance chilled him. Julia had been cold. He didn't want their son to be so cold.

But there was ice in Josh's voice when he said, "You're probably smart, Dad. Why ask Taylor to stay? She'd probably say no. There's nothing around here worth staying for. I can't wait to leave myself."

Seth moved forward, thinking to put his hand on the boy's shoulder. But Josh shrugged away and went into the cabin, slamming the door behind him. Seth

started after him, but then stopped. His son was confused. He needed answers about sex, about right and
wrong, about the possibility of love that lasted. But
Seth would be a hypocrite if he tried to take on those
questions.

For the first time ever, he doubted his wisdom in
bringing his son to live with him. Maybe a man like
him, a skeptic and a cynic, was the last person who
should have raised a child. He had wanted so much to
give Josh a life different from his own. But as Taylor
had said, he had merely created a son in his own image.

The way Josh had looked at him, had talked about
his relationship with Bobbie Jo, made Seth see himself for what he was—bitter, selfish, a user. Soon,
probably when she got away from here, Taylor was
going to regret what had happened between them.

But until then . . . God forgive him . . . until then, he
couldn't resist the sweetness she offered. Maybe he was
using her just as he had used Bobbie Jo and other
women. But to ask for more was just too big a risk.

Chapter Ten

"... I know I've let Dad down. But I never thought he would be so angry. I never thought I'd lose his love. But it's gone now, lost...."

Taylor stood beside the sheet-draped easel, smiling at the four people who were ranged about the cabin's small living room. Millie, whose broad face beamed with encouragement as she poured champagne into waiting glasses. Gerald, who looked proud. Josh, who was strangely somber. And Seth, who stood a little to the side of everyone else, just as Taylor would expect of him.

With more dramatic aplomb than she had ever used in her life, she cleared her throat. "I know you all may think I'm silly for doing this this way, but this piece of work is very important to me. I want it to be important to you.''

She paused, clasped her hands together and continued, ''This spring, my father handed me a diary. He might not have realized it at the time, but it was a little like giving me a ticket for an important journey. Through the diary, I found out things about my mother—and my biological father—that I might never have known otherwise. And then the diary led me here.''

Her gaze settled on Gerald. ''I found a grandfather who I love.'' She smiled at Millie and Josh. ''And friends who are more like family.'' She looked at Seth. ''I found more than I ever thought to dream of.'' Not wanting to spoil the moment with tears, she turned back to Gerald. ''Grandfather, this is my contribution to Austin Eagle Lodge.'' Carefully she drew the sheet from the easel.

Their expressions said it all. Wonder. Pride. Awe. Surprise.

Gerald came out of his chair and toward the drawing like a man in a daze. He stood, his fine hazel eyes seeming to roam over each line and curve.

Taylor slipped her arm around his waist. ''So, is it right?''

He started to speak, shook his head, then finally found his voice. ''It's Alaska,'' he whispered. ''The Alaska that Sarah and I discovered all those years ago.''

Taylor knew no critical acclaim or financial success would ever bring her the joy that came from her grandfather's perceptive words. He hugged her. "Thank you, Taylor." He drew away and tenderly, in the familiar gesture her mother had so often used, he smoothed the hair back from Taylor's forehead. "Thank you for the eagle. But most of all, for this summer."

The two of them shared a last, long look before Gerald released her to Millie's enthusiastic hug. Josh seemed tongue-tied and shy, but Taylor hugged him, too. Only with Seth did she hang back.

He had stepped closer to the drawing and now stood, with head cocked to the side, in a deep, thoughtful study. When he said nothing, Taylor had to demand a response. "Well?"

In his eyes was a look she couldn't fathom. "Now I see what you meant this afternoon about your other work."

So it wasn't her imagination. "Do you really? Can you see the growth, the change?"

"I'm no art critic, but there's a difference, a definite difference...." Again his gaze went back to the eagle. "He's powerful."

"I have to take him to Chicago."

Her statement drew the attention of everyone in the room.

"I won't take him for good," Taylor hastened to add. "He belongs to the lodge. But I can't do that exhibition without the drawing."

"But someone will want to buy him," Millie protested.

Taylor shook her head. "There's not enough money in the world to buy this from me. But he's got to be at the center of my Alaska work. I have other drawings that I have to finish. I can't wait to get to work on them. I can't wait until the gallery owner sees them. This is my best work, my very best, ever." In her excitement she took Seth's hand and squeezed it between her own. "I'm so glad I came here this summer. You all influenced this work."

Gerald picked up a champagne glass and lifted it high. "I'd say that's reason enough to drink a toast." When everyone had a glass in hand, he said, "To Taylor, who has given Eagle Lodge more than just this work of art."

A half hour of merriment followed, with Josh coughing over his first taste of champagne, Millie laughing in her robust way and Gerald beaming with pride. Seth remained a little distant, continuing to study the drawing thoughtfully.

Duty called of course. There was dinner to serve, a kitchen to clean, details to be taken care of for the next day's activities. Two of the lodge employees had the night off, so Taylor pitched in to help Millie, as she had done several times in the past. It was late when she finally found herself alone with Seth on the lodge porch.

Heaving a contented sigh, she leaned her head against his shoulder. "What a great day. Even scrubbing the pots Millie won't send through the dishwasher wasn't as much drudgery as usual.''

His arm went around her almost automatically. ''Soon you'll be the toast of the art world. You won't miss catering to a bunch of tourists.''

She chuckled. ''Believe it or not, I like most of the people who come through here. They're from so many places, and they all expect to find something different here. It's fun to hear what they think of our place.''

Our place. The words mocked Seth. This would never be her place. The lodge might appeal to her sense of adventure for a summer or even two. But not for more. She would eventually stagnate here. One glance at the eagle she had created told him she was meant for big things, great things. Her summer here might have inspired the work, but he wasn't naive enough to think it would hold her here.

Something akin to desperation seized him, and he said, ''Let's go to Juneau tomorrow.''

She looked at him in surprise. ''Tomorrow?''

''There's more to Alaska than trees and mountains. Juneau is the state capital. I have to fly a couple of guests in. Come with me. We'll stay the day, look around, have some fun.''

A smile began to curve her lips. ''You mean, just you and me, all alone, all day?''

''The city will be a good change.''

''Being anywhere alone with you will be a good change.''

From now until Taylor left, he was certain Josh was going to be scrutinizing their every move more closely than ever. His son was very angry about what they had discussed this afternoon. And Seth suddenly wanted Taylor all alone, all to himself, instead of sharing her with anyone else.

It was raining hard the next morning, a cold, steady rain that promised no letup in the foreseeable future. Despite the weather, however, Gerald insisted on walking down to the dock with them. The guests' belongings were stowed, and they were settled in the second seat of the larger floatplane.

"Take care of my favorite artist," Gerald told Seth as he hugged Taylor. "I think I'm going to commission a bear to hang across the room from the eagle."

Taylor kissed his cheek and scrambled into the plane.

Seth shook his hand. He thought Gerald looked more tired than usual this morning. He had been feeling so well for the past weeks that Seth had gotten used to not worrying. Now he had some guilt about going off for the day. "You take it easy," he admonished his old friend. "Everything should be okay around here today. The bookings from the cruise ships are light, and everyone's working, so—"

"Just get in the plane," Gerald interrupted. "You've got a pretty girl waiting for you. Go have some fun."

"If you're sure—"

"Go." There was plenty of command left in Gerald's voice.

Seth obeyed. He taxied the plane to the center of the river, took off and then circled back, dipping his wing in salute to the fast-diminishing blue-coated figure that waved from the dock.

Despite living nearby for fifteen years, Seth had never played tourist in Juneau. But after seeing the guests off at the airport, he and Taylor took the van back to the office and sloshed through the rain to the Alaska State Museum, visited the State Capitol, lunched on burgers and fries at a fast-food restaurant and spent hours wandering from one souvenir shop to another.

Taylor took advantage of the telephone in the lodge's Juneau office to call Joe. From what Seth could hear she and her father had a lively conversation, filled with details about her plans for the exhibition. That reminded Seth that she would be leaving, but he tried his best not to dwell on it. He had her with him today. That's all that mattered.

They stored her souvenir purchases at the office, and late afternoon found them with a gang of rowdy cruise passengers, enjoying the live country band at the Red Dog Saloon. A modern version of the frontier saloons made popular a century earlier, the Red Dog featured cold beer, sawdust on the floor and wildlife trophies mounted on the wall.

More interesting to Seth than anything else was the joy Taylor seemed to take from this return to civilization. He realized he should have brought her here before.

Taylor loved the loud music, the lights, the colors and the people out for a good time at any cost. But she was soon yearning for a quiet dinner alone with Seth. That's what today had been for, to be alone together, to talk. They could do neither at the Red Dog. Seth, however, seemed to be anticipating her every thought. The intimate, candle-lit restaurant where he took her to dinner was just the setting she wanted.

Charmed by the view of the harbor and the coziness of their surroundings, she smiled across the small table at him. "Do you realize that aside from picnics, this is the first meal you and I have ever eaten alone together?"

"There are a lot of things we've never done."

She grinned. "That sounds interesting."

He put his hand over hers where it lay on the table. Softly his thumb stroked across her knuckles. "If I didn't have my heart set on the New York strip I just ordered, we'd go check into a hotel."

Though pleased and secretly excited by the suggestion, she darted glances at nearby diners to see if they had heard.

Seth laughed, but kept his voice low. "You're something, you know. You get ideas in a machine shed with my son and your grandfather wandering around, but you're embarrassed at the thought of strangers eavesdropping."

"Call me perverse."

"I'd call you beautiful."

She was struck by the intensity of his gaze, but her denial was automatic. "I'm not beautiful."

"I think you are."

Her fingers threaded through his. "Then that makes me feel beautiful."

"You look like you belong here."

"Oh, now, stop it," she said. "I've got on the same blue jeans and pink sweater that looked great while I washaving a burger earlier."

"Candlelight does something for your eyes."

His teasing, romantic banter was a surprise. "I think I like what this place does for the way you talk, Mr. Hardy. We'll have to come back here."

Instantly, the warmth was gone from his face. She didn't know what could have been wrong with her suggestion, but he retreated from her. He released her hand, sat back and drained his drink. And when he looked back up, his gray eyes were as cold and remote as the rain-filled sky. But his tone was light, almost careless. "You're going to Chicago, remember? In three weeks, I think you said."

She shrugged. "Then we'll come here when I get back."

His eyes narrowed. But all he said was, "Yeah, we'll have dinner here when you get back."

And suddenly Taylor thought she understood. She touched his hand again, made him look at her. "I don't want to go, Seth. Really, I don't. But I have to go back if I'm going to get the exhibition together."

"Sure," he said. "It's no big thing."

The arrival of their food cut off her reply, and when the waitress had departed, Seth made it clear the subject of her impending departure was off limits. He talked about everything else, and after dinner, he seemed in an awful hurry to get back to the plane.

"What's the rush?" Taylor asked as they hurried along the waterfront in the rain.

"Fog," Seth muttered. He put a hand on her elbow to help her around a puddle. "It really rolled in while we were at dinner."

The fog was so heavy that Taylor couldn't see the lights of the buildings and houses across the harbor. Those had been perfectly visible just hours ago when they came out of the Red Dog.

At the office, they discovered the floatplanes carrying cruise passengers had made an early return, just in time to dodge the low clouds and swirling banks of fog. A discussion with one of the pilots and a quick radio message to the lodge dissuaded Seth from trying to take off.

The office staff left for the day, but Seth and Taylor waited around for a while. Soon it was apparent the fog was only growing thicker. Finally Seth stopped his pacing and said, "I guess we're going to be stuck here for the night."

Taylor couldn't be unhappy about something that would guarantee an entire night with Seth. She had never snuggled with him under warm covers. Never fallen asleep in his arms. Never watched him come awake in the morning. Tonight, thanks to the fog, they could do all that and more. She had to smile. "I never thought I'd like fog, but..."

Across the room, Seth sent her an answering understanding glance. The look in his eyes solidified her anticipation, sent excitement winging through her. "Just think," she murmured. "You didn't have to give up your steak to get me in a hotel."

Seth got on the radio to notify the lodge of their plans. Then he called around to find a hotel with a vacancy. He found one within walking distance, and soon they were hurrying through the rain again. The hotel was housed in an older structure, built around the turn of the century and fully restored. Or so the clerk at the front desk said. Discreetly, he made no comment when Seth told him they had no luggage. They were so intent on each other, on the room where blessed privacy awaited, that neither of them spoke as they hurried up to the third floor.

The door barely shut behind them before Seth was kissing her. In fact, they stopped just inside the door, ignoring the bed she had been craving earlier. Clothes were discarded. Kisses and touches made urgent demands till Seth lifted her up. Her legs went round him, her back was pressed to the door as he plunged into her.

Taylor spared half a thought to the people who might pass in the corridor outside. Then everything was lost but the movement of Seth's body against her own. And worry about who might hear them was forgotten. Overwhelmed by pleasure, she cried out, the sound echoed by Seth's own harsh groan.

He began to tremble, his knees to buckle. Ever so slowly they slid together to the floor.

All she could manage to say was a soft, "Thank God this door had no splinters."

Seth's laughter was weak. They practically crawled to the bed, where Taylor discovered the ultimate pleasure of falling asleep wrapped in his strong, warm embrace.

He woke her a few hours later. The bedside clock said nearly midnight. The curtains, which they had neglected to draw, revealed a world still shrouded in fog. All was clear inside, however. Seth's lazy kiss made his intent crystal clear. With hands, lips and tongue, he aroused her by small degrees, bringing her to a slow, deep completion, a tame counterpoint to the storm that had overtaken them earlier. Only when she was shuddering down from the crest did he slip inside her. And the climb started again.

Later, knowing they should sleep but reluctant to waste this rare interlude, they showered together. Hands slid, lingered on skin made sleek by soap and warm water. Their intent was intimacy more than arousal. They stayed under the cascading water for a long time. And this time when they went to bed, they pulled the curtains, enclosing themselves in a dark, secret world.

But Taylor knew reality was waiting outside somewhere. She could feel it hovering. Perhaps that's why she felt compelled to invite it in.

When Seth's arms closed around her, pulling her back against him, she had to murmur, "It could be like this, Seth. Forever."

She felt him stiffen. "You're going to Chicago, Taylor. I'm staying here."

"The planes fly both ways, you know."

"But you belong someplace else."

"How can you say that? I love it here. And I love you."

His doubts vibrated through the silence.

She waited, breathless in the darkness, wishing he would say he wanted her to be here with him, that he *needed* her to come back, that he loved her.

But Seth was silent.

She closed her eyes, fighting unreasonable tears. She should have known he wouldn't say he needed her. From the beginning he had made it clear he didn't really need anyone. She had come along and forced her way into his life. She knew she brought him joy, but he still couldn't admit his need. He had learned early in life to condition himself against that sort of need. He had hardened his heart to love.

She wished it weren't so important for him to love her. If it weren't, she might settle for what they had now. They could go on, drifting from day to day. She would have his passion, but not his love and certainly never his trust. But dammit, she wanted it all.

Her pride had always been strong, but she cast it aside now. "I love you, Seth Hardy. That's a fact. You can't avoid it, you can't wish it away. I'm not giving up until you admit you feel the same way for me."

With a heavy sigh, he rolled away from her and onto his back. She did the same. The bodies that had just been curled onto each other were now ramrod straight and not touching.

"Love is a fairy tale," Seth said at long last. "You should know that better than most, Taylor. Your mother went off chasing love, and look what it got her."

"She didn't give up, though. She found Joe."

"She got lucky."

That angered her. "It was love more than luck, Seth. And it was hard work, too. Relationships don't just happen. You have to work at them, work hard."

He was silent again, inches away from her in the dark, yet retreating from her rapidly.

Taylor's chest was tight with hurt. "I wish I could give you the guarantees you seem to need. But loving someone doesn't come with guarantees. I wish I could guarantee that I would always be happy here, that I would never miss Chicago. But I can't. I'm pretty sure that I would always be happy wherever you are. I'm willing to take a chance that I'm right. If two people love each other, they're willing to take risks. Love doesn't leave room for doubts."

Still he said nothing. She closed her eyes. "If you loved me, you'd know that I'm coming back after I go to Chicago." She paused, waiting in vain for an answer. Then she spoke her greatest fear aloud. "Except maybe you don't want me to come back. Is that it?"

He spoke slowly, each word striking her like blows. "Coming back or not is your decision."

Crushed, she turned on her side, away from him. His words proved that the past few weeks had really changed nothing between them. Her mind whirled, trying to think of a way to reach him. Even now, she had hope. Sooner or later, Seth would have to admit his true feelings.

Seth could feel her hurt. It took every ounce of strength he had not to reach out to her, to give her the reassurances she wanted. But he couldn't lie. Not to Taylor. She was so young, so full of optimism. Right now, she felt as if love would make everything possible. He knew how she would feel when she realized the emotion was only an illusion. Yes, he was unwilling to take risks. But experience had taught him too many hard lessons.

So he lay in the dark, unable to give Taylor what she wanted.

Taylor woke to partial darkness and a vague feeling of unease. It took her a moment to orient herself. Seth's arms were around her. In sleep, they had bridged the gap their conversation had made between them.

She was unwilling to think through their problems yet again. The clock showed it was later than she normally arose since having come to the lodge. She was surprised that Seth still slept. But she closed her eyes and tried to sleep again herself.

She had dreamed of her mother last night. A vivid dream in which Holly and Gerald were standing in the forest together. They had been at the eagle's nest. The bird, the eagle Taylor had drawn, had been soaring into the air. And Holly had been laughing. It was strange how vivid Taylor's memory of her mother's laughter was. But she had been so happy, laughing up at Gerald. Taylor smiled, thinking of them together.

The phone rang, and Seth woke up, snatching the receiver out of its cradle before it could ring again. He spoke his name, then sat up.

His harshly indrawn breath made Taylor sit up, too, clutching the sheet to her breast. She flipped on the bedside light. And Seth looked at her, his gray eyes full of agony.

And she knew.

She knew what her dream had meant.

But Seth was still on the phone, his expression darkening as he listened to whomever was speaking. He said, "I'll be right there." But instead of hanging up the phone, he closed his eyes and bowed his head.

Taylor found her voice. "Gerald's dead, isn't he?"

Seth nodded. "Millie just radioed the office and asked them to find us." He shut his eyes again. "But that's not all."

What else could there be?

"It's Josh. He found Gerald this morning. And then he took off in the plane." Seth opened his eyes. "It's that radio again. That damn radio. Josh isn't answering their calls."

Chapter Eleven

"...I didn't know what I was losing until it was gone. Someday, maybe I can make it right...."

It was twelve hours of hell.

Numbed by Gerald's death, Taylor had to sit half the morning at the office and watch Seth pace. The fog was still too thick for the floatplane to take off. Radio contact with the lodge reported there was still no sign of Josh.

When the fog began to lift, there was the silent flight over the mountains. Taylor could feel Seth's grief, his fear for his son. But she didn't try to reach him. He had a shield around him that was as thick and impenetrable as steel.

He landed at the lodge long enough to leave her on the dock and get a report. Then he was off again to look for Josh.

And Taylor faced other duties.

Millie, who had always been so calm and so capable, was devastated. So it was Taylor who had to ask one of the employees to radio for the coroner and an undertaker. Arrangements had to be made to bury Gerald beside Sarah here on the lodge property. Taylor had to keep her wits about her and attend to the lodge full of guests, too. The employees were all good people, but everyone was reeling from the shock of Gerald's death and the worry over Josh. They needed someone to be in control. Taylor had to be the one.

She wanted to go somewhere alone to cry. But there was too much to do. She knew she had to carry on with business as usual. Gerald would have wanted it that way. This lodge had been his life.

Perhaps it was good that she was so busy. She had no time to stand, scanning the skies for a glimpse of Seth's or Josh's planes.

The authorities joined in the search late in the afternoon. They were hampered by the lingering fog and a steady rain that had begun just after lunch. An ashen-faced Seth flew in, refueled and refused the food Taylor offered. She heard him tell the man in charge of the official search that he had gone to each of the places he thought Josh might have gone, each of his and Gerald's favorite spots. He had seen nothing. The man tried to get Seth to stay at the lodge. He refused and took off again.

Afternoon became evening. Taylor ran out of duties and sat on the lodge porch with Millie, waiting. Each minute stretched into hours. Once more she longed to talk to Joe. She had called him this morning from the office to tell him about Gerald and Josh. He and his wife had offered to get on a plane and come to Taylor. She had asked them to wait. The woman who ran the Juneau office had promised she would call Joe the minute Josh was found.

The jubilant radio call came in just before nine o'clock. Josh had been found.

Taylor and Millie donned slickers and stood on the dock, waiting, their relieved tears mingling with the rain. A rescue squad plane soon landed, and Josh climbed out. He looked pale and shaken but unharmed.

Millie swept him into her arms before he could take three steps. "You scared us, you did, boy. Scared us good."

His arms closed around her plump figure. "I'm sorry," he muttered. "I didn't mean to cause so much trouble." Over Millie's shoulder, he looked at Taylor. "But when I went down to the eagle nest and found Gerald...found him like that..." He squeezed his eyes shut. "I just had to get out of here."

"It's okay," Taylor told him. "It's really okay."

Josh went from Millie's embrace to Taylor's. He kept saying he was sorry. They stood in the rain, crying together until Seth's plane landed.

Pulling away from Taylor, Josh straightened his shoulders and wiped tears from his eyes. She could feel him steeling himself for a blow.

When Seth opened his plane door, when he actually saw his son standing safe and sound on the dock, he went weak. In two strides he had the boy in his arms. It was so good to feel him. Strong and alive. Still here. During this long, frantic day, he'd had too many hours in which to think of the worst. Gerald was gone. That was bad enough. Seth couldn't have survived the loss of his son, too.

But once the relief was over, the anger set in. Seth knew it wasn't the time for questions, but he was so tired, so overwrought, he couldn't stop the fury that spread through him. He set his son away from him and demanded to know what had happened.

It was the same old story. Once again Josh hadn't checked the radio. He hadn't even checked his fuel level. He had flown out of here like a blind man. It was only when low fuel forced him down in a secluded cove that he realized his radio wasn't working again. He had tried to make repairs, had sent up a few flares, but it had taken most of the day for help to find him.

"You did a damn fool thing," Seth told him.

Josh just closed his eyes. "I'm sorry."

"Do you realize the manpower that's been wasted out here looking for you?"

Taylor stepped in. "Seth, this isn't the time—"

He ignored her. "Josh, do you know what you've put us through? For the second time this summer—"

"I said I'm sorry." Tears were glimmering in the boy's eyes. "I just couldn't believe Gerald was dead. I had to get out of here."

"You should have stopped to think."

Taylor took Seth's arm but he shook her off, looking at Josh. "What do you have to say for yourself?"

Defiance shone through Josh's tears. "I'm sorry," he muttered, his face setting into hard lines. "I'm so sorry for letting you down. But this morning, all I knew was that Gerald was dead. And all I wanted to do was run. I wasn't thinking. I'm not as cold as you are, Dad. Sometimes I *feel* something." The boy's face twisted with bitterness. "How long has it been since you *felt* anything, Dad? How long—"

"That's enough," Seth cut in. "This isn't about me."

"You don't ever want to hear the truth about yourself, do you?"

"I said that's enough." Seth couldn't stand the pain in his son's face another minute. He couldn't stand the pain in his own heart, either. At the moment, he understood the impulse that had sent Josh flying off in the fog. For he wanted to go away, too.

Gerald was gone. The knowledge hit him anew. And guilt tore at him. While he had been in Juneau, in Taylor's arms, Gerald had been dying. He should have been here. His duty, the things he was supposed to protect were here.

He had to leave. He had to go somewhere to deal with his guilt and loss.

He turned on his heel, but Josh held him back. With the strength of a man, a strength that surprised Seth, his son made him turn. And his words hit like punches.

"I hate you."

Millie's cry broke in, "Oh, no, Josh. Don't say that. Oh, Seth, he doesn't mean it—"

"But it's true," the boy insisted.

"Josh . . ." Millie implored again. "Josh, please don't."

Seth didn't wait around to hear more. He strode off through the rain, blindly, moving more by instinct than sight. It was only when he reached the edge of the trees that he realized Taylor was with him.

"You've got to go back there," she said. "You've got to talk to your son."

He shook his head. "He's too upset."

"You're damn right he's upset." She grasped Seth's arm, made him face her. "He's hurting, Seth. He needs you to understand. I don't know why you had to attack him—"

"He's got to learn to think. If he lets his emotions rule him forever, he won't survive long."

Taylor stared up at him, her face streaked with rain, her eyes wide. "I can't believe you could talk this way about a sixteen-year-old boy who has just lost one of the most important people in his life."

"That doesn't excuse—"

Her voice rose. "For God's sake, Seth, he's the one who found Gerald this morning."

Seth closed his eyes. "Taylor, the boy has to learn—"

"Stop it," she screamed. "Just shut up and listen to yourself. You're worried about teaching him lessons when he's just faced the hardest one of all. What's wrong with you? Didn't you hear what he said to you?"

"He didn't mean it," Seth said, bleakly, hoping he was right.

But Taylor had no optimism. "My mother said she hated Gerald, too. Those words kept them apart for the rest of her life. That can't happen to you. Dear God, Seth, for once in your life reach out. That boy needs you."

Seth held up a hand for her to stop, but she kept on, telling him what he had to do. He couldn't deal with this now. He had to go, had to find a way to get past the knowledge that Gerald was dead. "Stop it," he said, grasping Taylor's arms. "Just stop. Don't tell me what I have to do. Right now, I—"

"But you've got to listen to me."

Something snapped inside him. He shook her. "Dammit, Taylor, just stop. Stop telling at me what I should do, what I should feel. From the minute you got here, that's all you've ever done. But now you have to stop. Stop trying to make me over into the person you think I should be."

With a strangled gasp, she pulled away. Her voice softened. "Seth, that's not it . . . I just want . . ."

"Yeah, *you* want," Seth muttered. He didn't know why he wanted to hurt her, but he couldn't stop himself. "You want something I don't have, Taylor. Maybe when you figure that out you'll go home. Where you belong."

"But this is home."

"No, it isn't. Now that Gerald's gone you can leave anytime. In fact, I want you to leave." Unable to stand the shattered look on her face, he turned and left her standing in the rain.

Taylor knew Seth was speaking from loss and pain, but he had told her to leave before. Just last night he had refused to ask her to stay. Over and over again, ever since she came, he had made it clear she didn't belong. Oh, she had fought her way into his life. She had won small victories. But she hadn't wanted to face what he had told her all along. She didn't want to face it now.

So she waited. Through the night, which she spent with Josh and Millie, the three of them clustered together for comfort, she waited for Seth to come back, to tell her he was sorry, that he didn't want her to leave.

But he didn't.

Even at the funeral, he said nothing more than the perfunctory words of grief. They stood on one side of the grave in weak sunlight, with only Josh and Millie between them, but separated by a world of differences. For a moment, Taylor regretted refusing Joe's offer to come and be with her. She would have liked a shoulder to lean on.

An eagle flew over them, his call echoing around the clearing. The breeze blew cool, drying the tears on Taylor's cheeks. She was comforted by these things of nature that Gerald had loved.

But from Seth came no comfort at all.

He seemed lost in misery. The distance between him and Josh was wider than ever. Seth went about the lodge like an automaton, his jaw more rigid, his shoulders held straighter than ever.

Millie told Taylor to give him time. "He feels things deep," she said. "Too deep for words."

Taylor already knew that. But she waited. And nothing happened.

A few days later, the two of them took a nearly silent trip into Juneau to see Gerald's lawyer. The will was very clear. There were bequests to Millie and Josh. But he had left Eagle Lodge to Taylor and Seth. They were equal partners.

On the dock when they got back to the lodge, Seth touched Taylor's arm. "Listen . . ."

She turned to him, her unsinkable hope surging to the surface. "Yes?"

"I'll buy you out," he said.

Her heart crashed. She heard him talking, but nothing registered. He couldn't be serious.

When he had stopped talking and stood looking at her in a perplexed manner, she said, "I could never sell."

"But you can't want the lodge."

The anger swelled through her. "As someone near and dear to me once said, stop telling me how I should feel."

He flushed, but insisted, "Taylor, be sensible. Let's talk this through."

In answer, she left him standing on the dock and went to the eagle's nest. On the large, flat rock, she waited, her legs curled beneath her, until the bird flew into the small clearing. Was it her imagination or did the creature hover a moment longer than usual over her, just as he had often done for Gerald?

Taylor took a deep breath and closed her eyes. As had happened so often this summer, she could almost feel her mother's presence. Gerald's, too. She wondered what they would tell her to do.

She couldn't sell, of course. No matter that she traveled far and never returned, Holly had loved this land. How could Taylor sell this place, even to Seth who loved it as much as Gerald and Holly had?

But she couldn't stay here, either. Not with the way things were between her and Seth. Maybe someday...

She didn't even try to complete the thought. Her usual hope was gone.

She sat on the rock for a long time, until Josh came to join her. He seemed despondent, his shoulders sloping, looking so much like his father that her heart ached.

He tossed rocks toward the river for several minutes before he said, "You're going away, aren't you?"

She nodded. "I think it's best."

"I'm leaving, too."

Taylor grasped his arm, made him look at her. "That's crazy talk. You're not going anywhere, except back to school in about two weeks. You stay in Juneau during the week for school, don't you?"

"Yeah, but—"

"That'll be good. That'll take your mind off things."

"But I'll have to come home every weekend."

"You'll be glad to see the lodge, to eat Millie's cooking." She paused. "You'll even be glad to see your father."

He sat forward, chin in hands, looking glum. "I didn't really mean what I said to him, you know."

She patted his shoulder. "Have you told him that?"

He shrugged. "You know me and Dad—we don't talk."

"You have to try, Josh. I know he didn't mean the things he said to you that night, either. He was just so upset, so sad about losing Gerald. You should make the effort, keep trying to mend the fences."

"Couldn't you mend the fences with him, too?"

Oh, if it could be as simple as Josh's trusting brown eyes made it seem. Taylor sighed. "Unfortunately, Josh, when it comes to matters between a man and woman, things get really complicated."

"Gerald told me once that love was one of the most uncomplicated things in the world."

Taylor wished she could agree. But she was beginning to think Seth was the one who had the right philosophy. Maybe love didn't really exist.

* * *

On the seventh morning after Gerald died, Seth came awake with a jerk. He had dreamed the telephone was ringing, as it had a week ago. He passed a hand over his face and relived those first, horrible moments of pain. Then he realized something else had awakened him. His son stood at the foot of his bed.

"Dad, I've done something you might not like."

Seth rubbed his eyes with the heel of his hand and swung his feet to the floor. Since that terrible scene on the dock, he and Josh had barely spoken. Several times Seth had tried to say something, but he couldn't. He couldn't do much of anything these days. His brain felt too jammed with problems. Gerald's death. Taylor's hurt. His son's anger. Plus the usual, everyday problems. Now here was something else.

He looked up at Josh. The boy...no, Seth realized, that word no longer applied. His son looked more like a man every day. He was going to have to get used to thinking of him that way. Brushing a hand through his hair, he said, "Okay, Josh, what's going on?"

"I took Taylor to the airport at about four this morning."

So she was gone.

"Well?" Josh said. "Aren't you angry?"

Feeling numb, Seth shook his head. "I guess she had her reasons for asking you to take her in the middle of the night."

"She didn't want to say goodbye to you," Josh said. "She cried all the way there."

Seth didn't like to think about Taylor crying. But her tears would dry once she was back where she belonged.

"Dad?"

He looked up again.

"I don't hate you, you know."

Emotion clogged Seth's throat, made his voice rough. "I know that, son."

"But I do think you're pretty stupid."

"What?"

Josh's hands clenched into fists at his side. "She loves you. She's one of the best things that ever happened around here. Dad, if you let her go, it'll be worse than Gerald dying. Because she'll always be out there, somewhere. And I think that's worse than death."

Josh dropped an envelope onto the bed. "Here. She said to give you this."

Seth looked at the square white envelope for a long time after Josh left. Finally he had to pick it up and unfold the note inside.

I can't sell you my birthright. But I trust you to make the right decisions about the lodge. If we have any profits in the next few years, please use my share to send Josh to college. I think that's what Gerald would want. And please, put the eagle over the mantel, where he said it should go. Goodbye.

                                        Love, Taylor.

Love, Taylor.

The words twisted through Seth, joined by other voices from other moments.

Gerald's gentle, *"Don't hurt her."*

Millie's blunt, *"You need Taylor. You may not even realize how much."*

From Josh, *"Dad, if you let her go, it'll be worse than death."*

And finally, Taylor's ardent, *"I love you, Seth Hardy. I'll always love you."*

He had spent a lifetime listening to the voice of experience. It had curled inside him, hissing, "Don't believe. Don't trust. Don't love."

Maybe it was time to silence the beast.

Seth reached for his jeans, calling, "Josh. Hey, Josh, come here...."

Loaded with tote bag, art supplies and purse, Taylor bumped and excused her way down the aisle of the crowded plane. Since she had been on standby for this flight to Seattle, she was virtually the last person on the small commuter jet. Her seat was by a window, just beyond two men who were wearing fishing caps and frowns.

Mumbling apologies, she stowed the art supplies overhead and crawled over the men's less than accommodating legs. She settled herself and her belongings, then turned to the window. Soon Alaska would be far behind. The sadness was unbelievable. What was it her mother had written? Oh, yes, Taylor remembered, the words were *And I never knew I'd miss the mountains....*

But Taylor knew. She would miss those tall, snowy peaks.

She would miss the eagle's flight.

The smell of Millie's biscuits.

Josh's shy smile.

And Seth.

Yes, even though he was difficult, even though he didn't believe in love, even though he had hurt her, she didn't want to leave. She knew if he tried, they could make it right. If he would only try. . . .

A disturbance near the front of the plane made her look up. A steward came running down the aisle. The man beside her muttered, "What in God's name?" As he leaned out to see, Taylor did the same, but almost lost her balance at the scene that greeted her.

Seth stood at the front of the cabin. He was arguing, struggling with a security guard and the steward. "I have a ticket," he kept insisting, waving a rectangle of paper. "Look, I bought a ticket." Then he looked up and met Taylor's gaze.

Over long rows of seats they looked at each other.

Then she sent fishing caps flying. She fought her way down the narrow aisle, through the steward and the guard. Somehow she made it into Seth's waiting arms.

Angry voices swirled around them, but all she heard was Seth's, "Don't go. Please don't go."

"But, Seth—"

He crushed her protest with his kiss, then murmured, "I love you, Taylor. I'm ready to take that risk."

And that was all she needed.

Epilogue

Snow was falling fast and thick as Taylor stepped out onto the lodge porch. Christmas morning would sport a new coat of white on top of the half foot or more already on the ground. She smiled. Christmas snow was supposed to be magic.

The door opened behind her. Seth said, "What are you doing out here? It's freezing."

She snuggled deeper into her parka. "I'm going for a walk."

"No, you're not."

She turned, grinning at his imperious tone. On occasion, he still tried to play the tyrant. It was over a year since their wedding. The time had added some additional silver to his hair, a line or two to his face. But she liked to think these lines came from laughter.

Marriage to this man wasn't easy. He had his moods. They had weathered some storms. But she had taught him how to trust. He had filled her life with passion.

Their life together was as it was meant to be. Taylor's career had boomed after the Chicago exhibition. She'd had another in Anchorage this past fall. Shops in Seattle and Oregon were clamoring for prints. Everyone was prospering. In the lodge, Millie was making a Christmas cake. Joe and his wife, here for the holiday, were drowsing in front of the fireplace above which Taylor's eagle held a place of honor. Josh was filling out college applications.

And in the spring there would be a baby. Hers and Seth's.

Which was exactly the reason he didn't want her out in the snow. "You shouldn't be trudging through this stuff."

She had never felt stronger in her life, but it didn't hurt to humor the man. "Then go with me."

He grumbled some more, but slipped inside for his coat and donned his boots. They struck off through the darkness for the eagle's nest. Beneath the tree where that ancient nest reposed, Taylor laid a spray of holly.

"What's that for?" Seth asked.

Taylor only smiled. There were some things her sensible husband would never understand, so it was best not to tell him about those times she had sat beneath this nest and felt a closeness to her mother and grandfather.

Sighing, she turned around and leaned back against Seth. His hands rested on her stomach above their child as he nuzzled her neck.

"Thank you," he murmured.

"For what?"

"For showing me that love isn't a fairy tale."

She turned to kiss him, and above the nest, the eagle's cry rang out. Strong. Powerful. Lasting. The sound echoed their love.

* * * * *

NORA ROBERTS

Love has a language all its own, and for centuries, flowers have symbolized love's finest expression. Discover the language of flowers—and love—in this romantic collection of 48 favorite books by bestselling author Nora Roberts.

Two titles are available each month at your favorite retail outlet.

In April, look for:

First Impressions, **Volume #5**
Reflections, **Volume #6**

In May, look for:

Night Moves, **Volume #7**
Dance of Dreams, **Volume #8**

Collect all 48 titles and become fluent in

THE LANGUAGE of LOVE

Silhouette®

LOL492

FREE GIFT OFFER

To receive your free gift, send us the specified number of proofs-of-purchase from any specially marked Free Gift Offer Harlequin or Silhouette book with the Free Gift Certificate properly completed, plus a check or money order (do not send cash) to cover postage and handling payable to Harlequin/Silhouette Free Gift Promotion Offer. We will send you the specified gift.

FREE GIFT CERTIFICATE

ITEM	A. GOLD TONE EARRINGS	B. GOLD TONE BRACELET	C. GOLD TONE NECKLACE
# of proofs-of-purchase required	3	6	9
Postage and Handling	$1.75	$2.25	$2.75
Check one	☐	☐	☐

Name: _____

Address: _____

City: _____ State: _____ Zip Code: _____

Mail this certificate, specified number of proofs-of-purchase and a check or money order for postage and handling to: HARLEQUIN/SILHOUETTE FREE GIFT OFFER 1992, P.O. Box 9057, Buffalo, NY 14269-9057. Requests must be received by July 31, 1992.

PLUS—Every time you submit a completed certificate with the correct number of proofs-of-purchase, you are automatically entered in our MILLION DOLLAR SWEEPSTAKES! No purchase or obligation necessary to enter. See below for alternate means of entry and how to obtain complete sweepstakes rules.

MILLION DOLLAR SWEEPSTAKES
NO PURCHASE OR OBLIGATION NECESSARY TO ENTER

To enter, hand-print (mechanical reproductions are not acceptable) your name and address on a 3"×5" card and mail to Million Dollar Sweepstakes 6097, c/o either P.O. Box 9056, Buffalo, NY 14269-9056 or P.O. Box 621, Fort Erie, Ontario L2A 5X3. Limit: one entry per envelope. Entries must be sent via 1st-class mail. For eligibility, entries must be received no later than March 31, 1994. No liability is assumed for printing errors, lost, late or misdirected entries.

Sweepstakes is open to persons 18 years of age or older. All applicable laws and regulations apply. Sweepstakes offer void wherever prohibited by law. Prizewinners will be determined no later than May 1994. Chances of winning are determined by the number of entries distributed and received. For a copy of the Official Rules governing this sweepstakes offer, send a self-addressed, stamped envelope (WA residents need not affix return postage) to: Million Dollar Sweepstakes Rules, P.O. Box 4733, Blair, NE 68009.

ONE PROOF-OF-PURCHASE
To collect your fabulous FREE GIFT you must include the necessary FREE GIFT proofs-of-purchase with a properly completed offer certificate.

(See center insert for details)